# Writing from the Heart and Mind

## Stories and poems

by Beverly Boden Rogers

For Bev's students who became teachers, her adult students and writing group friends who discovered they could write well, and for her family, who will treasure these stories.

# Table of Contents

# FOREWORD

Beverly Boden Rogers has always had a way with words. The pieces in this book are a selection, mostly written as a student of writing and then a writing teacher and group leader. There is much more: many journals stored away, her writing as a yearbook and school newspaper editor, and as an outreach coordinator at the Florida Museum of Natural History in Gainesville.

For someone whose life is so intertwined with words, she is parsimonious. Her pieces are usually short and her words carefully chosen. Hemingway would nod approval.

Many of these pieces are autobiographical: indeed, in her biography after the stories, I referred the reader to the first of the four sections of the book, "Growing Up," as a starting point.

This is a collection of work by a fine writer whose main purpose has been to develop other writers, not to be published. It might be tempting to think of it as a loving husband's tribute to his wife. If I ever had a tidge of that thought, it was washed away on the tide of the marvelous pieces I found. I hadn't seen a great deal of Bev's work since I began to write myself. I always knew she was a fine writer; now, with ten years of writing myself, I realize "fine writer" was an understatement.

I feared at first that I wouldn't find enough material to make even a thin book. I began searching: her computer, a tub of hanging files in which she organized work for her classes, an overstuffed white notebook she uses in her current writing group, and a twenty-year-old CD that was only readable by an expert archiver. I found sixty short pieces that speak to her life and her writing craft. There are certainly more.

But why has writing been so important to her?

Early in her teaching career, her principal asked why she was having her second-graders write so much without correcting their spelling. "Thinking," she said. (I'm sure she was too polite to roll her eyes.) "Writing is thinking in a purposeful way. They know their letters and sounds, so I told them to invent the words they need. Spelling will come naturally, later." For her, it was that short, that simple. Like her sentences.

Here is her work and her passion. indeed, writing from both the heart and the mind.

John Rogers, November 2023

# Writing from the Heart and Mind

# PART ONE

# GROWING UP

# Very First Memories

The first thing I remember is my crib. I assume I was about a year old because I was able to pull myself up. I was standing, holding on to the top railing, when my grandmother (I think) came into the room. She stood at the side of my crib, coiling my ringlets around her finger. I think she was cooing.

Years later I asked my mother if the configuration of my room was as I remembered. She confirmed that my crib was not perpendicular to any wall, but turned 90 degrees in the corner. I can still see it.

I also remember sitting in my highchair. It was kitty corner to the kitchen table. I was probably around two. I remember being comfortable and happy. My dad was serving breakfast—scrambled eggs, I think.

My last first memory is my most treasured. I was younger than four because Bob wasn't born yet. It was winter—Christmas time. My parents decided to take us into Boston to see the Christmas light and hear the carols on the Boston Common, the wide—open area across from the majestic capitol building. I don't think I'd ever been downtown, but I was amazed at how big it was. I felt very small and held tight to mommy and daddy. I remember being dazzled, but it was the ride home that was most special.

I was beyond tired and very crabby. Mom decided to take me up front on her lap. She rocked me and sang *Silent Night* in a very soft voice just to me. I hadn't heard that softness before. I felt so loved and so happy and so comfortable.

Looking back on this memory makes me realize how special it really was. Mother was not the warm cuddly type. I don1t remember being held and sung to and cooed to ever again. No wonder I remember it so clearly. Needless to say, *Silent Night* is my most treasured Christmas carol.

March 12, 2018

# MANY NAMES – ONE WOMAN

I loved her; I hated her. I respected her; I dismissed her. I believed her; I doubted her. I honored her; I ignored her. I was in awe of her; I recognized her weaknesses. I looked up to her; I looked away from her. I tried so hard; I failed so often.

She was my mother: my "Mama," my "Mommy," my "Mom." She became "Mother" and finally, "Grammie." Five words, one person.

I have only a few recollections of "Mama." I can see myself standing in my crib reaching up for her. She twirled one of my ringlets lovingly. I remember being snuggled on Mama's lap as Daddy drove the family home after seeing the Christmas lights on the Boston Common. I was so excited, but so tired. I was nuzzled with love as Mama softly sang "Silent Night" into my hair. I remember sitting in my highchair near the kitchen table while Daddy whistled and Mama sang one of their old favorites as they made breakfast together.

When I was almost four, my little brother was born. While Mama was in the hospital for the prescribed two weeks, a highly recommended woman, who we were to call "Aunt Sally," came to stay with us. My older brother was in grade school and old enough to play outside with his friends. I was Aunt Sally's main victim. "If you don't dry those dishes, I'll put you in a cold bathtub," was one of her many threats. I couldn't even reach the dishes without a stool.

I was petrified. Marna and Daddy didn't rescue me, because they never saw the abuse, and I must have been too scared to speak up. When Daddy was around, Aunt Sally was charming and sweet.

Later, when Marna came home, she had to be in bed. I remember Daddy carrying her downstairs one night to have dinner with us – "sweet" Aunt Sally at the head of the table.

After Marna had been home for a while, she must have seen my fear or overheard the threats, and she must have understood, because Aunt Sally left quite abruptly. I remember this scary woman wanting me to kiss her goodbye. I refused to do it. I became Marna's girl. I hated when she was out of sight.

I don't remember having separation problems when I was in Kindergarten. Mama and all the neighbor mothers took turns driving us to and from "school" – an old mansion that housed only Kindergarten. I have warm memories of learning new songs and making new friends.

But I have nightmare memories of first grade. I hated having to leave home and Mama. I hated the long cold bus ride to school. I hated the enormous building that housed all those unknown big kids. Each morning I would cry and complain of a stomachache (I really did feel sick to my stomach). I sobbed. I struggled.

After letting me stay home in bed for a few days and taking me to the doctor, Mama was loving, but firm. She took me to school, went inside to my classroom, and there she left me. Luckily I had a very loving, understanding teacher who helped quell my fears, but I was always happiest at home playing school.

Separation anxiety followed me for many years, but as I became more independent, "Mama" became "Mommy." I was happy during the "Mommy" years. I was well cared for, well loved, and I was able to do and be what Mommy wanted of me.

When love became more conditional, "Mommy" became "Mom." I couldn't be good enough for Mom. The happy-go-lucky days were fewer and farther between. "Shame on you!" started to echo in my ears. I tried to conform, but I kept coming up short. I couldn't let my anger and frustration surface because Mom was stoic and expected the same of me. Emotions were always squelched.

Mom was ever the martyr. She had never been allowed to be her own person. How could she let me flourish? As I blossomed she became jealous. I was able to do things she had never done. I ran for Student Council president and was the first "girl" ever elected. I was able to go to college, something she had desperately wanted to do. Her parents did not allow it even though she'd applied to and been accepted at Hunter College in New York. She was 16. I was allowed more freedom than she had ever been allowed, but I was stifled com pared to my friends.

Sometimes Mom was downright mean. She didn't trust me. She didn't respect my thoughts and feelings. I'm sure she loved me but I know she didn't really like me. She'd be shocked hear me say that, but she was so disapproving – so bitter.

Those were very hard years for both Mom and me. I couldn't do anything right in her eyes, nor could she in mine. We tried, but we were never on the same page.

Lucky for me, I found Mr. Right. We married (I even screwed up my wedding, according to Mother) and settled far from home. I usually referred to Mom as Mother by this time.

But I missed her and I missed home. The farther apart we were the closer we seemed to get. I remember when Mother came out to help when Geoff was born. I felt so very close to her then. I went back to calling her Mom. I even slipped a few times and called her "Mommy."

It was Geoff s early years that brought on the 5th appellation. My mother became "Grammie," and she was Grammie to all of us until she died 30 some odd years later.

She was a wonderful grandmother! The kids adored

her. She was loving and fun. She could let her hair down with the boys because they weren't her responsibility. She didn't need to mold them as she had felt she needed to do with my brothers and me. She could love them unconditionally. She loved them for who they were and what they were.

Grammie was a very special force in the boys' lives. I marvel at and am thankful for their perception of my mother, their grandmother. To Geoff, Edward and James she was all the things that a good mother and a fabulous grandmother should be! Thank goodness!

Now, as a well-beyond-middle-aged woman, I see my mother in such a different light. Her parents, her husband and her society repressed her. She cared for others but not for herself. She was ever sacrificing. She didn't fight for herself. Hell, she didn't know she *could* fight for herself!

I see now that she sank deeper and deeper into depression as I was growing up. And she wasn't allowed to help herself – no drugs (except maybe alcohol) – no talking to friends or (heaven forbid!) a therapist. "You mustn't air your dirty laundry," my father counseled. "Pull yourself together!" "It's all in your head!" "Snap out of it!" We all heard these words whenever the boat was rocked.

So mother eventually slipped away. Slowly! First her mind and then her body. It took ten years. Ten nasty years. How awful it must have been for her. How awful for all of us! First she was forgetful, then she became suspicious. That was followed by years of anger.

She was lost inside her head. She didn't know me, or thought I was her mother. She railed against me for not seeing her very often, even when I had just walked down the hall and back again.

One day the boys (by then young men) walked into her room to find her watching the NBA draft. She watched a lot of TV toward the end but didn't know how to change the channel.

Those years made me angry too. And frustrated! And sad! I never really knew my mother. She never let herself be known. She was never allowed to know herself.

When she finally died, I could be nothing but glad. She had long since lost all her spunk, all her love, all her dignity. I don't think I even cried.

And I really haven't cried yet. I'm starting to see that I need to. It's taken my own dark fall into hellish depression to make me see what she could never acknowledge. That she had had her goodness, her intellect, and ultimately her love squeezed out of her. I'm starting to understand how repressed and depressed she had been most of her life.

Mother, I loved you. Mama! Mommy! Mom! Mother! Grammie! I love you! I'm finally ready to cry. For you. For me.

November 16, 2006

# GRANDMOTHER

Grandmother was a crusty old soul, and I loved her dearly. She wasn't the cuddly, sit—on—her—lap type grandmother. There weren't any of those touchy—feely clues but I definitely knew she loved me. She just wasn't a warm, fuzzy grandma—but I adored her.

One of her most endearing statements to me was, "Why, Bevahly, you have the most wondaful hayyah. It's just like crisp lettuce!" I felt deeply proud and profoundly touched. But to this day I cannot equate hair with crisp lettuce – or lettuce of any kind, for that matter. Crisp lettuce? Why would you want hair like crisp lettuce? Still, I never doubted that that was a true compliment.

Grandmother was portly – I think that was the kind way, in those days, of saying "quite overweight." She didn't seem to notice or care. She wore ample, flimsy dresses that I thought were beautiful – always light and airy – pastel colors. Maybe she wore dark clothes in the winter, but I didn't see much of her other than in summer so my memories are light and airy.

And she loved poppit beads. So did I! I guess they

came from the 5 and 10 cent store but to me they were jewels. She had them in several colors. I had such fun playing with them; I'd make all sorts of designs and lengths. I really did think they were wonderful jewelry and assumed that every woman with any taste wore poppit beads.

Grandmother would swim every day. "Swim" is not the right word. She'd say she was going to The Loop to swim, but what she did was bob. She'd wrap a filmy scarf around her head and walk out a little past waist high. Then she'd sit down and bob. Up and down, up and down. I used to try to bob with her on occasion, but it was boring and it was hard for me. I realize now that she had a huge advantage—her girth. I always equated "fat" with "heavy," and "heavy" with "sink to the bottom," but later, much later, I learned that fat is a great advantage in the water. Fat floats!

Grandmother never sat on the beach. She'd appear around 4:00, disrobe, and walk into the water in her "swim costume," as she called it. (She even wore her beach shoes in.) Then she'd bob contentedly for about 20 minutes. She'd stand up, walk back to shore, towel off and head home straightaway.

She didn't dig in the sand with her grandchildren. She didn't build sandcastles or drizzle sand forests. She didn't sail or boat with us although I do have a far distant memory of my grandfather's boat, the Cara, over at the island, so I assume she had boated in the past.

The stories go that grandfather did most of the cooking. I remember only a few meals at my grandparent's house. Thanksgiving, I think. The dining room was squashed full of people – great grandmother, all of us – maybe a couple of the Nickerson boys. My grandfather must have cooked those feasts. Dad said grandma couldn't even boil an egg and had no intentions of learning.

One time my parents did leave grandmother to care for us when they went off for a week. We were overjoyed when we had hamburgers three nights in a row. The 4th night of burgers was a bit much and when she said, on the fifth night, that we'd be having hamburgers again, I wangled an invitation to dinner at the neighbors. Their split pea soup with knackwurst was delicious.

Grandmother liked to visit us at our winter home. She had the "suite" on the third floor, and she was up there a lot. She'd go lie down after every meal, which I thought was just a grandmotherly thing. My mother, I realized when I got older, was mighty miffed not to get some help with the dishes.

Grandmother was fiercely proud of her Cape Cod roots and her whaling ancestry. She would get a faraway look in her eye. She'd tell us the stories she'd heard from her grandmother—about the whaling voyages of her grandfather, Cap'n Nickerson. She would tell how her grandmother had traveled with the

Captain a few times. It was those stories that instilled in my grandma that burning desire to see the places they'd seen. Her wanderlust was one dimensional – to go to Hawaii and see the whaling village there. From the residuals from <u>The Cut of Her Jib</u> she was able to fulfill that dream. She booked passage on a freighter – no fancy cruise ship for her. She had a compact little cabin, ate with the crew and was "happy as a clam at high water" as she would say.

Before she left on her voyage, she filled a jar with Cotuit seawater and took it off with her. After her freighter was well through the Panama Canal, she poured her precious Atlantic into the Pacific.

She spent 3 months in Hawaii. She had packed in one small suitcase. To this day, when I pack for a trip I wonder how on earth she managed in one small suitcase! We called her once in Hawaii. It must have been some special occasion because long distance phone calls were rare at my house.

She was content after that trip and I'm not sure she ever left the Cape again. She had been born in the big house on the hill in Cotuit. Her family decided it was too far from the center of town and built another house closer in. My grandfather built a house for his wife right next door to her family's home. Her brother and his boys lived behind on the next street. She outlived everyone, but her boys and their families were in Cotuit all summer and her nephews kept an eye on her the rest of the year.

These memories of mine are from the fifties. Grandmother died in 1959. I was 14. I've wished many times at many ages that I could have a conversation with her. Pick her brain. Know her adult to adult. She was just a grandmother to me. I'd like to know her as a woman, a writer, a friend, and an equal.

I realize now that grandmother was a woman well ahead of her time. She was liberated before the term was coined. She didn't do all the "womanly things. She didn't cook. She didn't sew. She read and she wrote. In her later years she tried her hand at painting. Today we'd say, "She did her own thing!" Go in peace, Grandmother.

August 31, 2000

# POLIO

When I was in the fourth grade, I was playing with my friend Mai when I got a sharp pain in my right arm. I complained to my mother, who commiserated. Mai's family took us to the beach, and we had a fine time. My arm didn't bother me much for the rest of the day. Then the pain was back, and my arm didn't seem to work. I couldn't write my name clearly. Our family doctor sent me to a specialist, who decided I had polio. Polio was a big thing back then. I was right-handed, so I had to "switch sides" to my left hand. I had to learn to eat and drink left-handed, brush my teeth left-handed, do most everything left-handed. I became pretty good at writing left-handed. To this day, I often drink left-handed.

After several months of special exercises, my right arm began to feel better, but it was weak. That next summer, polio became epidemic. Everybody assumed my diagnosis had been correct and so I was not going to get it. I was relieved and had a summer of not having to worry about polio.

In retrospect, I shudder at how lucky I was.

June 22, 2023

# My Summers in Cotuit

Cotuit has always been a very special place for me. I'm told that soon after I was born I was taken there to visit my Grandparents. Needless to say I don't remember that trip. I'm not sure what my first memory of Cotuit is.

I've always loved the picture of me sitting with Great Grandmother on the sofa, but I don't remember it being taken. I do remember her (Ina Nickerson) when I was still young. She was mostly bedridden by then, very old and very frail, but she loved sitting up when she could. She always held my hand when I visited. Her skin was so soft and white. I loved the feel of it. The last time I saw her was for Thanksgiving dinner at Gramma and Grampa's house.

My mother tells of her early married life when she and Dad would go down the Cape to see the family. Ina, his cherished grandmother had married the son of the whaling cap'n Horace Nickerson. He was one of the captains who raised the funds to build the Meeting House on Main Street.

Great Grandma was very religious and spent many,

many hours at the church. She believed that Sunday was the day of rest. When mother was visiting and started knitting, she was told to put her project away and rest. After that whenever Mom and Dad were on the Cape on a Sunday, Mom's knitting would be nowhere to be seen, but it miraculously reappeared on Monday.

# BACK TO SCHOOL

The day school ended, we left our Weston home for Cape Cod. We had said our goodbyes to our school friends. I had spent a lot of time figuring out what things I wanted to take and which I could leave behind. I would not be in Weston and see my friends until summer was over, even though it was only an hour and a half between places.

Cape Cod was a different world than Weston. Beach every day, clams being dug for father's afternoon martini hour, good books to read. We reconnected with friends from Shaker Heights, Washington DC and, well, all over. Most of our days were spent on the beach. I had a job babysitting two adorable children almost every day. At noontime, I took them back to their home and left them with the maid, who would feed them and put them down for naps. They would be ready for me when I went back at 2:00, and off we went to the beach again. In the evenings, my friends would come over my barn and play ping pong or tell ghost stories. Every now and then there would be a square dance, and we'd enjoy the music and learning the patterns of the various dances. Because we danced barefoot, it was a chore to get out feet clean to get into bed. That in itself was fun.

Once a week, we went over to Oyster Harbors (very posh), where a professional ballroom dancer would teach us how to dance the foxtrot, waltz, and samba. Quite different than Spike Jones on a scratchy square dance record. My parents would sit having cocktails, watching us.

Toward the end of August, friends began to leave. Little by little we all went back to our homes. It was hard to say goodbye to my summer friends. The goodbyes were sad … much more difficult to leave the Cape than when we left Weston. Summer was over. School beckoned.

# MR. FROST AND
# MORNING PUZZLES

I have always loved jigsaw puzzles. There was a bookstore in Wellesley Hills near our home that had puzzles you could rent. My mom would rent one for me now and then.

I would get out the card table, dump out the box, turn over all the pieces, collect the edge pieces. I always started with the edge because it made the puzzle take shape. That was important, because the rented puzzles were usually wooden and had no picture, just the name of the puzzle like "the Meads" or "Out on the Ocean." Getting the edge in place was necessary to define the scene.

No one in my family cared much for doing puzzles, so I worked on them alone. One summer the Frosts from Shaker Heights, Ohio, rented my uncle's barn. Mr. Frost loved puzzles, too, and always had one going.

While his wife and kids slept, he would work on a puzzle. He invited me to join him after 7:00 AM "to puzzle!" I loved those mornings with Mr. Frost.

We had great talks, and we completed many puzzles. He, a grownup, talked to me, a young girl of twelve, with respect. I loved both our conversations and the puzzles.

# JACK FROST

The Frosts, a well—off family from Shaker Heights, Ohio rented my Uncle's "barn" in Cotuit for the summer, every summer. It was across the street and two doors up from my summer home. Mr. Frost had a profound effect on my life.

He loved jigsaw puzzles, the real thing. The wooden ones you rented at the bookstore in Hyannis. Mr. Frost was never without one. They had no picture with them, only a title: Sunrise over the meadow, Pulling for Victory etc.. There were specially shaped pieces and easy to recognize edge pieces.

Mr. Frost set up a card table in the living room and invited me to join him "anytime." I took him at his word and showed up around 8:00 one morning. The door was unlocked, so I walked in and called his name. I'd obviously gotten him out of bed, but he wasn't angry. He made a cup of coffee and joined me at the card table while his wife and kids slumbered on. I was 7 or 8, but I was really good at "spatial relationships" Mr. Frost told me. He liked sitting with me and working together. We really had a good time getting all these puzzles together. When one was finished, he'd make a trip to Hyannis and get another. He also told me I *was* welcome to come in anytime but, if no one was up yet, just sit down and work on the puzzle.

Sometimes on hot, steamy nights Mr. Frost would wake up his kids and my Dad would wake my brothers and me and we'd all go down to the Loop Beach and for a dip. We loved swimming with the phosphorescent jellyfish and had a hard time believing we swam with them during the day, too.

Mr. Frost had a marvelous map of Cape Cod. I often told him how much I liked it. To this day it is my favorite of all Cape Cod maps. It was a line drawing in brownish black ink on off white paper. It was large—32x26. I really admired it, and often told him so.

At some point the Frosts stopped spending their summers in Cotuit and all us kids grew into adulthood. Our families stayed in touch.

They were on the Cape for my wedding in 1963. I didn't see them again until several years later when John's cousin got married in a Cleveland suburbs.

We rented a car and drove to Shaker Heights to visit the Frosts.

They were delighted that we'd made the effort. And treated us (and our new son, Geoffrey) with kindness and love. Just before we said our goodbyes, Mr. Frost said, "Wait! I have something for you. He reappeared with a long tube. In it was a rolled up copy of his Cape

Cod map. When I threw my arms around him we each came away with a tear in our eye. I never saw my favorite adults again.

Mr. Frost always treated me with respect, even as a child. I had abilities he admired and he let me know it. He was kind and generous man. He was the epitome of what any young girl would like an adult to be. And what this grown woman hopes she grew into. Thank you, Jack Frost!

February 2018

# THE MOVE

*(For Mary and Audrey on their move to a new house)*

When I was eight my parents decided to buy a different summer home. I really loved our house and didn't want to move. It had been built by a whaling captain. It was like the one my great-great grandfather had built for his bride in the 1880s. The "new" house was nearby and it too had been built by a whaling captain. The house we were buying was already furnished, so my parents left our house and its furniture for the next owner.

I loved my "old" room. It had a plain, old ordinary closet, but the back of the closet had a secret door that led into the turret. We loved to play in there and watch the people outside through the wonderful windows.

My room also had an old bedside table that had a drawer that could be locked by a beautiful, heavy brass key. I wanted to move that table to the new house, but Mom and Dad said no. So I left the drawer unlocked and took the key. I treasured that key. I didn't tell anyone that I had it until many years later. Yes, I guess it was stealing, but I didn't think the new owners would know it even existed and therefore wouldn't miss it.

As an adult, I knocked on the door to that wonderful old house and was invited in by the owner. She led me all through the house and even let me go into the turret. I told her about the key and she chuckled.

To this day, I still have that key! I've treasured it long, long ago and I treasure it still. Remind me to show it to you some day.

# MY BACKYARD

I had the best backyard ever. All the kids in the neighborhood considered it their backyard too. All of us lived on Glen Road* in Weston, Massachusetts. To get there we had to go down a little hill past my family's chicken coop. I don't remember the chickens since I was born after the war, but my older brother does. He told me the chickens would get out every now and then and he'd run after them to try to catch them. Funny! I've heard Mom had a wonderful vegetable garden back there too. Mom was pretty industrious.

Well once down, we would go up a little rise and there was our incredible backyard in all it's magical glory. To the left was a huge apple orchard. In the spring it smelled like perfume when all thirty or so trees were in bloom. And in the fall the trees were heavy with apples. They looked pretty good from a distance but you wouldn't want to eat one. They were full of worms.

As an adult now I try to imagine our backyard as a working farm with various crops and animals. The farm owners were the Warren and Davina Jennings. They lived two doors down from us and were really good friends with my parents. We kids adored both of them too. The other Jennings lived right next to us on the other side. They were very reclusive and didn't like children. Hard to believe that the old-stick-in-the-mud was Warren's brother.

But, back to the Backyard. Way to the right there was a dirt track that passed a bunch of falling down barns. We were told to never play near the barns, and we had no urge to. Davina had the most delicious vegetable garden back there. She was usually out there working in this massive garden when we kids went by and she always offered us a carrot or a bean.

As we walked along the path we would come to an old house that wasn't lived in but had a great set of steps that became a comfortable place to sit and rest before going on. Once back on the path it turned and went past a deep stone quarry. We'd look down into it but we never tried to play there, either. Past that was a pine forest where we could cool off and get out of the sun. Farther along there was an opening into a pasture. Someone who lived in a neighborhood that abutted the "backyard" at this end kept his horse in there. Sometimes we'd take a carrot out to her.

From the middle of the pasture looking back in the direction we'd come, we could see the old barns and our Glen Road houses. If you wanted to drive to the houses beyond the pasture it would take awhile and be a least two miles. I doubt we'd walked even a mile—half a mile maybe, but we didn't worry about distances back then.

Sometimes we'd just retrace our steps to get home but if we were in a sporting mood we'd head back. It was a challenge from the pasture and we weren't supposed to go across the stream other than on the plank bridge, but . . . sometimes we'd cross on the big, huge grassy humps that poked up throughout the waterway. It wasn't deep, but if you slipped off you went home with soggy socks and smelly shoes. I never fell in but my cousin did when she was visiting us. She didn't get in trouble but I sure did!

Up a rise from there and we'd end up in the massive fields. Not sure what the farm's crop had been but it was a grain of some sort – maybe wheat or oats, etc. In the fall the "grass" was straw like and matted easily. We'd make houses by stomping out a living room, a bedroom, etc. Lots of make believe.

We spent a lot of time in the "backyard." Even in winter we would put on our bear claw skis and ski the trail or up and over the fields. I never played out there in the summer because my family left for the Cape the day school let out and didn't come home until the day before school started again at the end of summer.

March 19, 2018

*   When you rode your bike down Glen Road to its end you'd be at Route 16 in Newton Lower Falls. The Boston Marathon goes along there on its way to the end in Boston.

# THE LIE

Penny Brown had carrot red hair, a brother named Charlie, and a father who scared the wits out of me. She was a year older. She was very self-assured, and I admired and feared her at the same time.

Every June my family left home and headed to the Cape for the summer. At Penny's insistence, I begged and pleaded with my parents to let Penny visit. And visit she did.

One day she and I picked several roses off the fence between Mrs. Fox's house and ours. Mrs. Fox had felt it necessary to erect this ugly (except for the roses) fence when it became apparent that the noisy Boden children and their friends might mar her postage stamp size yard. It was true; occasionally a stray ball may have landed beyond our property line or, in the heat of a fine game of tag, we may have stepped out of bounds.

Mrs. Fox was my first living witch. She was always tsk-tsking us as she wagged her bony finger.

One year, between summers, she erected a fence. It was an ugly fence and seemed unnecessary, but it wasn't a surprise. The roses, however, did help. So when Penny suggested that we pick some I said, "We can't. They're Mrs. Fox's!"

"Not the ones on your side of the fence!" replied Penny.

I didn't argue in the face of her wisdom. We picked a few soft, pink flowers, enjoying their rich smell. But soon we tired of the thrill of having plucked them and discarded them in the nearby field.

After lunch Penny and I were up in my room when we heard a knock on the front door, and then Mrs. Fox's voice as she scolded my mother for having such ill behaved children. Mother must have said some soothing things, and soon Mrs. Fox headed home.

Mother called up the stairs, "Beverly, did you pick Mrs. Fox's flowers?"

Penny nudged me and whispered, "Say no!"

Lying was something we never, ever did when I was a kid. (We learned how later from the same adults who'd taught us not to lie—but that's a different story.)

"No." I called down the stairs.

And then mother betrayed me. "You're lying!" she said. "I saw you pick the roses earlier. You will stay in your room for the rest of the day thinking about that. Then she added, "Penny, come down now and we'll go to the beach."

I know I never forgave Penny. And I'm not sure I've ever forgiven my mother, but I do know that I only pick flowers occasionally and that when I do, they're mine to pick.

# PART TWO

# ADULTHOOD

# MY FIRST ... AND LAST ...
# BLIND DATE

Let me start with some background. All through high school I was madly in love with Steve. He was it! Happily ever after and so on. But he graduated 2 years ahead of me, and off he went to college.. and fraternity parties... and the world beyond home and high school. Dumping me was a long, slow, agonizing process. So much for happily ever after!

Because of Steve, most of my friends were older than I. Linda, my best friend, had been at Radcliffe for 2 years when I finally left home for college. Dick, Linda's boyfriend since 8th grade, was at Dartmouth. Linda and Dick stayed in my life even though Steve went on to bigger and better things. In the fall of my freshman year, Linda called to say she was going to Hanover and would I like to come. Dick would set me up with a date.

Dick drove down and picked us up on Friday afternoon (I forgot to say that my roommate, CeCe hitched a ride at the last minute) and we drove the three and a half hours to Hanover. Dick talked most of the way. First of all "someone special" had had to cancel at the last minute and Dick had asked several brothers if they'd like a blind date. As he told it, John had said, "Sure, what the hell." Dick told him to watch his mouth. And to be a gentleman. And to dress appropriately. And to be respectful. And... and... and. As I listened to Dick I thought "good grief, this guy must think I'm some sort of saintly prude." By the time we got to Hanover I was pretty damn unhappy.

Well, on with the story. Dick led us up the walk to the big red door of the Sig Ep house and gallantly held the door for the three of us. We stood in the vestibule as someone called up the stairs, "Hey, Rogers, your date is here!" Was that an "oh, shit" we heard come down the stairwell?

It was followed by a tall, unshaven, scruffy, galoomph—Rogers. He was dressed in dirty khakis and a cut off, faded, Dartmouth sweatshirt. He bounded down the stairs, walked into the already too crowded vestibule and proceeded to bow and introduce himself to CeCe. Dick then made introductions. When John realized his gaffe he neatly stepped back to bow to me. Unfortunately he hadn't seen the wooden rake leaning against the wall. His heel caught the tines of that old rake, and it came up and hit him squarely and firmly on the back of his head.

"Oh, good grief!" I thought. "A whole weekend of this?"

Oh, shit, whaddid I just hear? "Rogers, your date's here!"? Damn, I gotta watch the time better.

Must have fallen asleep. That's what I get for pulling an all-nighter. Well, that paper had to get done. It's due tomorrow. I wonder if she'll want to go to class with me in the morning. Doubt it, she doesn't sound too bright.

I guess I have no choice but to go down this way. Unshaven! Definitely messy after band practice in the drizzle. Well, take me as I am, young lady. Oh, my god, there's Tabors and Linda, a nice looker . . . and a dog. The dog, that must be my date. Oh well, it's only a weekend. Only?!

Things didn't get much better. We drove down to Lebanon and ate at an interesting restaurant. I was introduced to pita bread that had been opened and grilled with butter. Very delicious. John and I spent little time talking to each other but I was impressed with his vocabulary, his brains and his humor as he carried the conversation around the table.

Then it was back to the Sig Ep house for a party. We were all down in the basement. The music was loud, the conversation shouted, and there was lots of beer.

John was taking a shot at the pool table while I sat on a nearby bench and watched. A brother, Mosher (apparently fraternity brothers only know last names) came over and sat next to me, and in his over served way began flirting. Well, Mosher wasn't my type—for one thing he was too short! Anyway, when he realized he was getting nowhere he said, "Are there any more like you where you came from? Can you fix me up?" I allowed as how I could and proceeded to write down my phone number on a cocktail napkin for him. John seemed oblivious. Mosher finally moseyed off.

I seemed to surprise John when I said I'd really like to go to his classes in the morning. "Heck," he said, "why not?"

And so I climbed the stairs to the dorm style attic room in the Occam Inn and fell asleep easily despite the comings and goings of the other fifteen or so girls I was sharing this room with. Not as bad as I expected I thought as I went over the events of the day. I guess I will make it through.

Jeez, that girl sure is a flirt—with everyone but me. I think half the brothers are in love with her already. Well, I'll just play it cool. I don't need another heartbreaker in my life. I left Rockford, and soon after my high school squeeze left me. That hurt. I'm not about to be blind sided again any time soon!

Party's still going strong here, but I need to put the finishing touches on this paper and get some shuteye.

I slept like a baby despite the comings and goings of several girls in various stages of happiness, sleepiness and drunkenness. Was bright—eyed and bushy tailed (as my dad always said) and waiting downstairs in the sitting room at the appointed time–8:00. By 8:15 I was beginning to feel like I'd been stood up. By 8:20 I was getting ticked. At 8:25, when John showed up, I was not pleased. The breakfast he had promised was not going to happen; we grabbed a couple of donuts at Lou's and headed off to his 9:00 writing class held in an anteroom in Baker Library.

The class was small—no more than 10. The professor was a wee, wiry, sartorial looking gentleman. His students looked the part too. The guys wore jackets and called the professor "Sir." He, in turn, called his students by their formal names. "Mr. Rogers, I see you've brought a young lady this morning. Welcome, miss. And now, sir, would you please start us off by reading your paper."

Several papers were read that morning and each was dissected by the professor and his students. The constructive criticism was brutal. Most of the writing was good.

There was little time for chit-chat as we headed to

John's Shakespeare class in Dartmouth Hall. This class was large and I wasn't the only female in the crowd. We found seats together but sat silently because of the din around us. When the professor walked in, precisely at 10:30 the room fell silent. I chuckled to myself as I thought of the proverbial "pin drop." Suddenly Shakespeare came alive. Both John and I took note as Professor Smith introduced Shakespeare's characters through recitation and description. You'd have thought he knew each personally and intimately. I was enthralled and decided that the weekend was a success no matter what was yet to come. I was glad I was just a visitor, however, when the assignments were dispensed. Memorize many passages (several hundred lines, I guessed) to recite and/or transcribe during the next class. "To be or not to be…" I would find it hard to be a Shakespeare scholar!

I felt awed and excited as we walked out into the cold but sunlit New Hampshire day. I didn't mind that John reached for my hand and held on as we walked toward Main Street to find some lunch. We talked Shakespeare and poetry, writing and literature. We were comfortable.

But then the real world intruded again. John needed to have me seated in the band section at the stadium and then run off to be ready to march in with the band at 2:00. Could hardly ask for better seats—40 yard line. I sat with the other "band dates" and took in the sights and sounds. The Dartmouth side of the field faces the mountains. I would have loved to have seen them a few weeks before—at peak fall colors time, I mused. On this mid October week—end they still showed various shades of rusts and ocher. How beautiful. How enduring. How calming.

Calming! The noise! Students and older folks—alums I presumed—were filling into the stadium. You could feel the excitement, the anticipation. game was exciting and great fun. The band struck up often and I got swept into the loyalty and heritage that is a Dartmouth football game. I did learn that I had to be careful of the guys right behind me; those trumpets need their spit valves cleaned often!

*(This fragment was recovered from a damaged CD;*
*The balance was lost in extraction. The piece itself is*
*slightly edited.)*

# THE PERFECT NIGHT

"A soft fall rain slips down through the trees and the smell of the ocean is so strong that it can almost be licked off the air."

Sebastian Junger, *The Perfect Storm*

They slip out after dinner and head for that smell – the ocean. He has never been here before. He doesn't know the sea; he grew up in the Midwest. She loves it here; she has spent every summer of her eighteen years in this place. She wonders what his reaction will be. They both know this is a test.

They have put on foul weather gear, always hanging in the den closet, ready for anyone braving the elements. He may feel uncomfortable in the rubbery, yellow slicker, but she thinks he looks rugged and handsome.

They have known each other only a few months. Their meeting was an arranged deal and each had been uncomfortable. . Both were coming off old, hurtful relationships, and they are wary, to say the least. They were unprepared for the chemistry that threatened to overwhelm them.

They have seen each other several times since that first meeting, but they continue to fight the chemistry. They joke about it. The laugh about it. They think they can slough it off. Each is holding back. And now he is here, meeting her family, sharing her special place. They walk to the beach in silence. The wind is picking up. The rain is coming down in earnest. They hold hands and walk in the dark, blustery night—tense and relaxed at the same time.

Here is the beach. They are together in her favorite spot in the whole world. This beach!. She wants him to love it, and she's afraid he won't.. She's afraid! She wants this to be perfect.

They sit on the seawall tasting the salty water as it drips off their yellow hoods. Together they marvel at the size of the waves. He can't know how unusual big waves are at this beach. She tries to describe to him this calm peaceful bay, but all they see is how churned up and angry the sea is with the oncoming Nor'easter.. She feels that healthy fear of the elements. What will this landlubber think, she wonders?

He says he wants to walk on the beach. She's impressed and jumps off the wall into the hard, rain soaked sand. Usually so soft, she thinks. He follows her, grabs both her hands in his and swings her round and round. Their laughter is swallowed up by the wind and rain and roar of the waves. She leads him down the beach pointing out the boulders that are a part of each jetty put out so many years ago. She knows the size and shape and color of each of these rocks from countless trips over them in the past. He navigates the rocks carefully but without trepidation; he doesn't falter despite the starless, moonless night.

Up ahead is the bluff. They can barely make it out high above the beach. It's a tricky climb up the rocks, but it is the very best spot on this stretch of beach. Should they risk it on this windy, stormy night? They climb slowly, each checking that the other is okay, and when they get to the top they are very alone and very together. The world is dark and powerful but oh so beautiful. They stand with their arms entwined looking out toward the angry sea. He turns to her, holds her face in his hands and shouts against the wind, "It's time I told you!" He bends close and whispers, "I love you!"

Her smile transforms her face, her eyes sparkle. "Oh, yes," she counters, "And I, you!"

They marvel at the joy, the love, the chemistry. It truly is a perfect night.

September 27, 2000
Edited March 24, 2017

# THE PARTY

The party was to start at 6:00 – in honor of her birthday.

("The old battle-axe!)

It was now 3:00. John had been commissioned to take the boys off to the local petting zoo. She'd even given him an extra $30 so the boys could buy a souvenir.

("Does money buy happiness?")

My boys adored her, their grandmother.

I was seething, but I pasted on a smile as I did as I was told. Polish the silver! Dust the living room! Bring the folding chairs up from the basement! Etc.

("Never a please.") But I smiled.

When my family returned a few hours later, the boys raced past me to their grandmother's open arms and proudly showed off their new zoo sweatshirts.

("Oh goody! I'll be reminded of this trip every time I do the laundry!") I smiled.

"I want you to tell me all about your outing," their grammie said to the boys. To me she said, "Join us when you finish with the silver, Beverly."

("She could just as easily have called me Cinderella.") I smiled.

At 5:00 the caterers arrived. Thank goodness. Mary treated them as if they were the guests. "Let me take your coats." and "May I get you something to drink?" and so on. "What a dear, gracious lady" they remarked to me.

("Tyrant is more like it!")

"How lucky you are!"

"Oh yes." I replied, "How lucky." And I smiled.

I hardly had time to clean up for the party but I was without harassment for an hour while she luxuriated in the bath. I polished up the boys and helped them into their new, grandmother-bought, seersucker suits.

("I'd sure love that $200 to get them some practical clothes.")

Finally I put on my new dress. The one I'd finished the night before at 2:00.

When Mary saw me she asked, "Where did you find that Dior?"

"I made it" I answered.

("With zipper, $28.50.")

"Oh, that's too bad," she dismissed.

("If you turn your dress inside out people could read your label!") I smiled.

The party was a smashing success. The food was delicious, the drinks ever flowing, and the hostess was the centerpiece. All evening I had people saying things like, "It must be such fun having Mary for a mother in law." and "She makes a party seem so effortless." Or "She's so generous, interesting and kind."

("Not to mention demonic!") I nodded and smiled.

When the last guest left and the caterers had been complimented and paid, the three of us sat in the living room with our feet up rehashing the night's events and its great success. Finally, as Mary climbed the stairs for bed she called over her shoulder, "Oh, by the way Beverly, thanks for all your hard work. Good night."

("Slave driver!")

"No problem. My pleasure." I replied. And I smiled.

Later, in bed, John said, "I can't tell you how many of the old guard sought me out tonight to tell me how charming my wife is." He hugged me and said, "This may have been mother's party, but you were the belle of the ball!"

I smiled – a genuine smile.

July 2000

# THE LOOP BEACH

The Loop Beach is a very special place. Always has been, always will be. You can go down to the water's edge, scoop up a bit and start digging where there is no water. And dig, and dig. And soon there will be water. It's like magic.

My friends and I would test that now and then. We'd go further up, then dig, dig, dig. And, sure enough, we'd find water. Magic!

We'd tell each other that if we went far enough, we'd go all the way to China. (Of course, we knew that wasn't true.)

One thing we learned was that no matter how far we dug, we had ... had ... had ... to fill up the hole before we left. A gaping hole was a hazard, a good way to break a leg.

The loop has been with me forever. What was once a cart path has been paved. The house my great-great-great grandfather built still sits atop a rise that looks across the beach and the entrance to Cotuit harbor so his wife could see the packet bringing him home from Nantucket. It is much modified now, expanded, air-conditioned. My grandmother found his journal in the attic, careful copperplate script preserved all those years. She made it into a book and used the money from its sale to travel to Hawaii to see the place the New England whalers put into port after the perilous journey around Cape Horn.

The rock jetty where John and I walked in the teeth of a Nor'easter on the first Thanksgiving after we met was buried for many years, attentive to the tempo of the sea. It has come uncovered now, a reminder of the place he asked me to marry him a year after that first Thanksgiving.

I have been to that beach every year of my life except for a couple. When we had children, we took our vacation in Cotuit. They went through that process of water discovery themselves, and were warned to be sure to fill, that someone might break a leg. We bought a home there, a quarter mile up from Loop Beach. We brought our family and their children there. And Robin, our much-loved cat, who would escort us on our evening walks to the beach, scouting our path, waiting for us under the beach plum bushes on the edge.

These days, we go to the home we owned, sold when it became a chore to keep, and now rent. Our grandchildren go to Loop Beach. To dig in the sand. Maybe to China.

# You Never Know

You never know what's going to meet you around the next corner. You think you've got your life in order. You think you have all your ducks in s row. And just when you're feeling safe and secure and in charge, you round that corner again.

You're sitting on the beach in your twentieth summer. You're happily daydreaming about the man you were to have married last month. You're disappointed that his mother intervened and convinced you that it would be better to put off the wedding until you'd both finished school. Okay, you can live with that. It does make sense. If only your parents would get off your back.

You're sitting quietly. You're alone. You're lazily watching the sail of a Sunfish pulled up on the beach flapping in the gentle breeze.

And then, around the corner, if there are any corners on a beach, you see a young man. He's gorgeous. You are struck by his casual good looks – his tall, lean, bronzed body. His blonde—tending toward red—curly hair. You are drawn to his dancing eyes and dazzling smile.

He approaches you, points to the Sunfish and says, "You any idea how to sail one of these bloody things?

You're charmed by his British accent and ready to teach the world how to sail. "Sure," you say.

"Care to join me?" he asks.

"Why not," you reply, amazed. How unlike you it is to talk to, let alone go off with a complete stranger.

You climb on to the flat, uncomfortable boat and catch the glint of sun off your engagement ring. You introduce yourself.

"Edmund here," he offers.

Once out on the water you realize that he knows enough about wind, water and Sunfish to do an okay job of sailing. There's little you can teach, but you are able to help him a bit with term. "That's called the sheet, not a rope," and "on a boat a rope is called a line," and so forth. Semantics.

You sail and chat and sail. You feel like you've known Edmund a long time. Finally you beach the Sunfish on the outer side of the island – a place you've never been before – and you wonder why. It's beautiful. Wilder than the other side. A bit rocky. More waves. You swim. You walk along the deserted shore and you enjoy the give and take of learning to know a new person.

You tell Edmund that you are engaged to a wonderful young man who will someday make you his bride. You explain how, at the moment, your fiancé is 1000 miles away, bowing to his mother's wishes. Edmund listens, raises his expressive eyebrows, but says nothing.

He tells you he's eighteen and off on an adventure – a trip around the world—with his parents' blessing. Amazing! you think. You find that he's staying with friends who are also friends of yours. You learn that he cares little for education but loves what travel can teach him.

He asks what you want from life, and you ponder, wondering what's the right thing to say – freedom? Truth? Because you pause he says, "That's an easy one for me. I want happiness." Don't we all, you think. How simple, how lovely.

You see a lot of Edmund over the next two weeks. You fall in love – not so much with the man/child but with his charm, his daring, his focus.

And you come to see that you must find yourself. You need to discover who you are and what you want out of life. You realize that you're trying to be what others want you to be – your parents, your fiancé, his mother, the list is long.

You give your engagement ring back when next you see your fiancé. You apologize for the hurt explaining that just by being attracted to another man you realized that you don't yet know what's ahead. You explain that you love him but being engaged for another two years seems wrong. You hate to see the pain your words cause, but you're sure it is the right thing for you. You know your future does not include Edmund, and you hope it will include this man you've hurt. But you will have to wait. You're sad, but happy to be pursuing freedom and truth. Happiness cannot come without these two you muse. And you wonder what's around the next corner.

# Engagement Broken Aftermath

It was the hardest thing I have ever done, and despite the sadness I am glad I had the courage to do it. I had broken my engagement to John after a long hard summer of being apart. I was mad at his mother for suggesting we postpone our wedding for two years. I was mad at John for agreeing with her, and I was mad at myself for my lack of understanding of myself.

It was done and now I had to carry on, to go forward. I hoped John would reach out to me some day, but after such a surprise, such a blow I wouldn't blame him if he decided to walk away from the hurt. I knew that all I could do was wait and hope.

I had planned to stay in the city for several says. John's mother had gotten three rooms at the Roosevelt hotel and we were all going apartment hunting, John needed a place to live while he was getting his Masters at the Stern School of Finance at New York University. I stayed only one night.

I left the next morning after returning our beautiful

ring. I don't remember saying goodbye to Mrs. Rogers. John put me in a cab to Grand Central. Both of us were crying. Then the taxi slipped into traffic and I was off. It was over.

On the train, I had a lot of time to think about my decision and to ponder where I'd gotten the strength to do what I'd done. By the time I reached Boston I was composed and dare I say, happy. I had taken my own life into my own hands for the first time – ever. I'd always done what everyone else wanted me to do. Now I felt I was ready to find out about me.

# SUCH AN AMAZING DAY

Today's the day. I hardly slept a wink last night. I'm so excited. The weather forecast is on our side, sunny but cool. What more could a girl ask for on her wedding day? I'm so glad we're having the wedding and the reception here at our beautiful summer home. We'll take our vows overlooking the water.

I must make a thorough list of all the things I need to do today. A list all the things that will need my attention.

    ..Go over all the lists I have already made.

    ..Wrap the bridesmaids' gifts.

    ..Check with the flower girl's and the ring bearer's Moms to be sure the kids know exactly what to do. So cute!

    ..Be sure that all the utilitarian operations are ready. Everything must be perfect.

    ..Be sure that the bartenders are set up and ready to do their thing.

    ..Ditto the coffee and tea ladies. Do they have everything they need?

..Make sure the cake has been delivered.

..Take a long, steamy hot shower.

..Shave underarms and legs.

..Fuss with hair.

..Take an hour of alone time.

..Have the flowers been delivered?

..Relax (well at least try).


"Okay, okay, Mom! I know. I've been over all of this a million times. But, I don't plan to ever have to plan for my own wedding again.

Yes, I will try to relax. Relaxing is a big order, Mom." The wedding was just as I'd envisioned it. Dreamlike!

Several hours later I was in the bridal suite with my new husband his arms were around me and he was cooing in my ear. The atmosphere was electric.

Hmmmmmmmm ....

January 20, 2019

# Affirmations

They had had a ritual each night as she tucked him into bed. "I love you." she would say.

"How much do you love me?" he would ask.

"More than the sun and the moon and the stars!" she would respond.

One night he added, "And the astronauts?"

"And the astronauts!" she replied with a chuckle of pure love.

From then on the ritual never varied.

As a small boy, whenever he needed assurance, day or night, he would ask, "How much do you love me?" And they would run through their question and answer sequence. As a teen, for the same assurance, he would simply ask, "And the astronauts?" She would smile and reassure him with an empathic, "And the astronauts!"

They live far apart now, but their repartee is not forgotten. She always signs a note, not with the usual, "Love," but with "More than the sun and the moon and the stars..." They end long distance phone calls in the same way.

So with all the celestial talk for all these many

years, you'd think there would be confidence and joy. There isn't. There's doubt and fear instead. Somehow this boy has grown into a man who looks at himself and sees failure. He says to himself, "I'm not good enough." "I'm not smart enough." "I'm not…" "I'm not…" "I'm not…"

She continues to love him more than the sun and the moon and the stars, but that's not enough anymore. The self doubt, the self loathing has taken over and instead of astronauts he now faces demons. He is afraid. For years he has hidden his fears in his counterculture. He has tried being arrogant. He has worked at being cocky. He has turned to booze and pot for solace.

Now his demons are unleashed. He has shut down. He can't leave his few safe places without fear; he's afraid he won't be able to breathe. He carries a paper bag with him at all times in case he hyperventilates. He can't eat in a restaurant. This fabulous musician has to force himself on stage for a gig. He struggles with being outside. He feels sheer panic when he goes to the airport. He even throws up.

But he wills himself on that airplane and he flies to his safest place, home. He has come to work on his demons. He knows he can't let them drag him down any longer. He has made that leap from darkness. He is with those he loves the most and he will work with a therapist for a month or two. Already he feels the worst is behind him.

She, too, is afraid. She wants only the best for him. She wants him to be healthy, self sufficient, self assured and happy. She sees the goodness in him. She sees the talent and the strength and the compassion. She wants to believe he can rid himself of his demons. She must believe!

She will continue to love him. She will continue to recite their childhood celestial affirmation with him. But now she will add to that repartee. She wants him to follow the advice of another great musician, Les Brown. He said, "Shoot for the moon. Even if you miss it you will land among the stars."

January 9, 2001

# WAITING FOR A WEE ONE

She's here. Missy Rogers is here! Ed finally called from the delivery room to say she'd been born about fifteen minutes ago. For a minute or so I could hear her crying in the background. She was seeing the world for the first time from her mother's chest. And soon, I too was crying – from pure joy, from relief, and from frustration at being so far away and therefore, so removed from this birth. The birth of my cherished granddaughter – my middle son's first child. What memories of parenthood, of hopes and dreams! Such a miracle is birth.

There are no particulars yet. No birth weight or length*. No name. They've told us all along that they have two possibilities, but they wanted to meet her first. I guess fifteen minutes isn't quite long enough to decide who she is.

Welcome to this great big, wonderful world, Missy. You're in good hands, cherished, loved, adored. I so want to meet you. Till then, I send my love,

Grandmother Rogers
July 26, 2005

*    Brother Bob chastised me. "You measure the *length* of a fish. You measure the *height* of a human."
"Not one who's lying flat." I replied.

# Mary's First Four Years

So you're four years old, Miss Mary. How you've grown. I missed so much of it – your first tooth, your first step, your first words. It's hard to be so far away, but I'm so thankful for the times I have seen you, been with you, seen your growth. Growth is so much more noticeable when there's a lapse of time, and that's been exciting.

When you were born I had a hard time calling you Mary. Mary Rogers was my mother-in-law and the name threw me. It seemed too old. It carried memories of the struggles she and I had trying to build a loving relationship. Your daddy and your uncles helped that relationship a great deal.

It's okay now. I love your name, Mary Elizabeth Rogers. There must be a thousand Mary Rogers in the world but there's only one Mary Rogers in my life now. I no longer need to call you Miss Mary, but sometimes I still do. I just find it endearing. It's always said with love and respect for my near perfect (no one should be perfect) granddaughter.

So what have you done in your four years? I know

the gist of it even if I haven't been able to watch all of it happen.

I've seen that you love and are loved, by your Mommy and Daddy, your Nana and Poppa, your Grammie and Grandfather, your aunts and uncles and all your cousins and extended family. Did you know you've been loved by your sister ever since the day she was born a little over a year ago.

I remember when I was with you when Audrey was brand new. You were so gentle and so helpful. Do you remember when you brought your lovey to her on the changing table when she was crying? You stood behind her and gently rubbed her fuzzy, tiny head.

I've seen how you love your home and everything in it. You love all of your books. How I love reading to you as we cuddle. I think you'll be a great reader – fluent and discerning. You love your dollies and all those stuffed animals. You love your new bed with its wonderful sheets. You love your toys, and unlike a lot of kids, you're very good at taking care of them and picking up before the day is over.

I've seen how you love the outdoors. Your backyard is a special place with its swing and sandbox and all those great outdoor toys. You love running and jumping and having your hair fly out behind you.

I've seen how you love the beach. Some of the very best pictures we have of you were taken at the beach. There's such obvious joy there. And the two beaches you are used to are so different. Your Pacific is cold and wavy and noisy. Your Cotuit beach is sheltered and shallow and calm. You love both and are lucky to know both.

I've heard how you love music and I've seen your interest in it. You have such a lovely voice. All your CDs and their special songs. You don't pound on your piano the way some little ones do. And you were so gentle with Grandfather's guitar whenever he took it out.

I've seen how you love to learn. You are comfortable in your school and have wonderful teachers and classmates. You learn while sitting with your peers, your parents, and even from Dora and Diego. You're very curious. It's such fun to see you experimenting with everything around you. Did you know that while you're playing you're learning?

What will the future bring? There is no crystal ball. We can only guess, but my guess is that you will have a joyous and fulfilling life. I see you surrounded by those who respect and love you. And I see you respecting and loving in return.

And remember, I'll always, always love you, no matter what.

Happy Birthday, Miss Mary!

Grammie

July 26, 2009

# TO BE A TEACHER

I always knew I wanted to be a teacher.

My dad found a real blackboard and attached it to the wall in our basement for classroom. I loved the feeling of chalk on my fingers. It was messy but wonderful. I had two real blackboard erasers, too. I set four of my dolls on chairs facing the blackboard and taught them how to add and subtract. I was very proud of my students.

My first-grade teacher, Mrs. Devereau, was my model. I had a hard time learning how to write her name. But all through elementary school I would stop by to say hi to her whenever I could.

I did become a grade schoolteacher and always loved it and remembered Mrs. Devereau when my past students would stop by.

In Illinois and St. Louis Park, I taught 3rd and 4th grade and loved the children at that age. I always concentrated on teaching writing because it both developed language and allowed personality to express itself.

In 1997, we moved to Gainesville Florida. I found

that I missed teaching, so I began work at the Florida Museum of Natural History, where I was an outreach specialist. I loved the work, which involved carrying two large rolling suitcases (very heavy) to schools and events. Inside were boxes of arrowheads, owl pellets, snake heads, and other fascinating treasures for hands-on science learning. While we were in Florida, graduating St. Louis Park seniors were asked the most influential teachers in their time in school. I was so deeply honored to be the only elementary teacher of the half dozen teachers honored.

In 2011, we decided to return to Minnesota. I was surprised and delighted that a group of my students from those long ago third and fourth grade classes asked me to meet to have lunch with them. What a special day! Seven young women had become teachers themselves. "All because of you, Mrs. Rogers." I thought of Mrs. Devereau.

It's been 56 years since I first taught. The joy of helping others learn never leaves one. Mothers teach, grandmothers love watching grandchildren blossom.

I ended up starting a writers group with adult friends. You can't really teach someone how to write, but you can offer encouragement and prompts and a good ear. We aren't looking to become published writers, but we certainly enjoy our time together.

June 15, 2023

# BREATHE

Breathe! All you have to do is breathe and count to ten. Many potentially bad things can be averted with this simple advice.

Breathe! All you have to do is breathe.

What does this really mean? Stop! Take a few seconds to access the situation and think clearly about how to respond. It's the thinking clearly part that really matters. The opposite of flying off the handle—reacting from anger.

There's often a thin line between discipline and abuse. I've stood on that line a few times in my sixty-plus years, and it is truly scary. I remember thinking, "So this is why children are abused." I'd never understood before.

Breathe! I learned this lesson way back in the sixties when I was first teaching. It had been raining for several dreary days that October in Chicago. My fourth graders were as antsy and logy from inactivity as I was. As their teacher, I was in charge of recess (no playground supervisors in those days), but of course, if you couldn't go outside, recess became a long twenty-five minutes in your classroom. The kids had some free time to read or play board games, but I knew we all needed to move, as well. There were several options: "Simon Says," or "Follow the Leader," and—the kids' favorite—exercising to Robert Preston's "Chicken Fat."

On one of these particularly miserable days the class decided on Follow the Leader and I was "it." In trying to keep the twenty plus kids moving, I was snaking through desks and around furniture.

Michael, a smart, adorable but bratty kid, had been cutting up all morning. Recess seemed to give him more courage. I finally had to have him stand behind me as we tried to exercise in our cramped classroom.

Michael just wouldn't let up. When he tried to trip one of his classmates as she snaked near him, I lost it! I snapped my body around with lightning speed, as a frog shoots out its sticky tongue to catch a fly. I was swinging at Michael, aiming to catch his arm—catch it hard, I must admit.

Well, Michael's instincts told him I was going for the jugular, so he ducked. I caught him right across the face. Whoop! It scared both of us! Michael, stunned, sat down quietly. His classmates were silent. I sent them to their seats, gave them an assignment, alerted.

the teacher across the way that I was leaving for a few minutes and went to tell the principal what had happened.

"Ah," he said, "Michael again! I'm amazed you haven't complained of him to me before this." (It wasn't so long ago that Illinois still allowed hitting a child.)

Several teachers in this building were trying to reform their discipline practices. But he did address the gravity of a teacher, me, hitting a student. He told me I must call the parents, explain the situation, own up to the fact that I'd made a mistake, and apologize for what I'd done. Now, that's punishment. But the punishment did fit the crime, I knew.

When the kids went off to gym—the only time during the day that I wasn't responsible for them, I called Michael's home.

Nervously, I told Michael's mother the story. I thought she'd be really angry, maybe offer to sue. I really didn't know what to expect, but I sure didn't expect what I got.

"I've been celebrating because it's been two months since school started, and this is the first call I've gotten from this year's teacher.

That's a record! Congratulations, my dear." Mrs. C said.

She went on to say that, of course, she didn't con-done what I'd done—which basically was to slap her child across the face. But she did understand my frustration with her child.

"He's not an easy one, that Michael. I can't tell you how many times I've had to keep myself from beating the living tar out of him. But who would that hurt? Or, more to the point, who would it help?" she said.

For most of my break, we talked about Michael and the things that had shaped his young mind.

"He was never able to talk about losing his older brother," his mother told me. He was only three at the time so his language skills didn't allow him to express what he was feeling. His actions were his outlet."

Mrs. C went on to say that she hoped that some day he would be able to understand his own grief. "But that doesn't mean it's okay for Michael to be a bully and a brat. Be tough with him, dear, but do not allow yourself to swing in anger.

"In fact, let me give you a bit of advice—for all the Michaels and the obstacles you will encounter as you go along in life. When you find yourself on the verge of losing it, breathe. Take a deep breath and count to ten. Remember, Breathe! Good luck, dear.

Michael and I ended up having a good year together. He knew I could and would get mad at him when he misbehaved. But he also knew, when I had apologized to him and told him that I shouldn't have let my anger get the better of me, that I really cared for him and wanted to help him become the best person he could be. That year Michael excelled. He and I worked to bring out the best in each other. I was able to teach him a lot and he, inadvertently, taught me a very important lesson that both of us used in our classroom and in life: Breathe!

December 14, 2007
Revised July 12, 2010

# THE PERFECT GOOD-BYE

James was there when his grandfather died. He heard the thud as he fell across the threshold. He saw the unmoving body. He heard the noises, the death rattle, as his beloved grandfather lay on the kitchen floor. James was thirteen years old.

At that moment he became the man of the house. He watched his grandmother's stunned silence and knew she wasn't able to function.

There was no 911 in Cotuit in the summer of 1991. It was James who found the emergency number. It was James who called for help. He was the one who answered the paramedics' questions. It was he who called his Uncle Rich who came over, and with Grammie, followed the ambulance to the hospital.

The crisis was over. Now all he could do was wait. Wait to hear what he already knew was true. It wasn't a long wait, but an hour can feel like an eternity.

James' friend, Andy, was there, and Aunt Pam had stayed behind to be with the boys. She was kind and comforting. Her calming presence helped to pass the time, but her talk of God's will and praying fell on deaf ears.

Finally, the dreaded call came. Grandfather was dead. Massive heart attack. One minute he was fine; the next he was gone.

James adored his grandfather. He looked up to him. He admired him. He loved him dearly. Theirs was a special relationship, a special bond. Being thirteen, James didn't see that the man, like all of us, had his faults. He drank too much. He was very manipulative. He was vain and overbearing.

But to James, he was a hero. He and his grandfather belonged to a mutual admiration society, and his grandmother would often sing that song to them. James loved his grandfather's zany jokes and incredibly bad puns.

He spent hours with him out in his cluttered but very impressive workshop in the barn He marveled at the crazy inventions his grandfather came up with. The gull sweep cut of PVC pipe had caused the man to cut a hole into the adjoining bedroom, so that the 30-foot length of pipe could be flat and straight as he sent it through the band saw. There was the pick he made so that he could get just one coffee filter off a stack of basket-style filters. Or the little wooden knob with felt on its bottom that would perfectly cover the saltshaker knob and holes so the salt was protected from the damp Cape Cod air.

*(This fragment was recovered from a damaged CD; the last few paragraphs were garbled.)*

# Rachel Taught Me
# Two Things

## (Names Changed)

Rachel taught me two things: you can't tell a book by its cover and... loosen up. Being a librarian, I certainly should have known the first. Having been brought up by stoic New Englanders, I could definitely use the second. I like to think that Rachel taught me well and that I was a good learner.

The media center hummed. There were three of us. The Media Technology Specialist – me – and two assistants. One kept the library in shape, shelved books, manned the check out desk, tracked down kids with overdue books, etc., and the other kept the equipment running smoothly. They freed me up to be creative and to teach. I was good at both; kids enjoyed being in the media center and in its computer lab. They ohhed and ahhed over the hundreds of new books I'd discovered and ordered. They enjoyed doing research both electronically and in print. They loved when I'd roll into their classroom with my computer on wheels and its projection system, plug into the network and make a spreadsheet with them. Or start a database. Or surf the Internet on a topic they were studying. My job was highly visible and lots of fun. Then my assistant, the one with the hardware expertise decided to be a travel agent instead.

I advertised in the Minneapolis paper. *Technology assistant needed.* I got many applications and interviewed several candidates. The pay did not jibe with the expertise needed, but there were still possibilities. When Jim, my principal, who'd already lost one very good teacher because of his ogling, came to me and said, "I think you should hire Rachel," I almost fell off my chair. Rachel! I thought, she hasn't even applied, thank goodness.

Rachel had been at Cedar Manor for a couple of years. She was the aide to Rosy, a girl in a wheelchair who needed constant help. My few dealings with her had been short but pleasant but I'd never gone beyond her looks. She was younger than I by fifteen years and very pretty, but oh, the outfits. She'd wear tight leather pants and a low—cut spandex top, or a mini skirt with a low cut ruffled blouse, or cropped leggings with a low—cut lace tee shirt. She looked like my idea of a middle class hooker. She was always just this side of acceptable. There was a hint of class despite the getups.

The process of finding a new assistant took several weeks and in the end "we" decided on Rachel. She knew nothing about technology and hardware. I knew only software and I needed someone who could keep all the machines, video cameras, microphones, digital cameras, overhead projectors, not to mention all the computers in the building – 35 alone in the Media Center lab – two in each classroom—working. Help! What a nightmare! I was baffled, angry, frustrated and scared. How would I deal with an untrained, unskilled, bimbette?

Well, Rachel was amazing. She learned fast and well and was an expert within weeks. (And she was able to ignore Jim the many times he happened to be strolling through the Media Center.) In this, her new job, she got more dressed up each day, but she still looked just on the edge of unacceptable.

Of all the people I worked with, teachers, administrators and paras (as the aides were called) the one I miss the most is Rachel. She was a horse of a different color, a breath of fresh air.

Here was a woman who knows what she wants in life. She doesn't really care what people think. She doesn't care about the things that are often too important to others. She's very insightful. She didn't get an education despite the fact that she is a very intelligent person. She is happy being a para when, with a degree, I'm sure she could have climbed the ladder of success. There's not a dishonest bone in her body. Jim (and many others, I'm sure) know just where they stand. She lives with a man, and I've no doubt she's faithful to him. She's an excellent mother to her two beautiful, wholesome daughters. Needless to say, I came to respect and love her – almost to revere her.

As I said, she taught me two very valuable lessons: don't prejudge and loosen up. I work on these lessons everyday, and I thank Rachel.

# MEDIA SPECIALIST

When I was the media specialist at Cedar Manor school I discovered Photoshop, a brand new product. I was smitten by its abilities and its possibilities. Soon after we moved to Florida and my advanced technology days were miles away.

Once there, I needed various family pictures cropped and printed. I wanted some color ones turned to black and white. That's when I discovered Digital Photo, a Gainesville store that specialized in working with photos. I started taking my film and my projects to them. I watched what the staff at the computers was doing, and I was blown away. There was a before and after album for customers to peruse. I was awestruck. There was a family portrait in which the matriarch's glasses caught the flash in a very disturbing way. The "artist" at the computer, Jonathan, gave her glasses flash free. There were two separate pictures of twins standing against a flowering wall. Jonathan put the twins together and made the background meld together. You'd swear the picture of the twins had been one the picture.

I kept asking the owner if he would ever give lessons in Photoshop. "Someday, maybe," he'd reply. I gave Digital Photo a lot of our business so was in and out often. Finally John, the owner, was so sick of me asking about lessons that we finally settled on one evening (after hours) a week. I loved working with the program and John. He was a good teacher and very patient. I worked on many projects from my hundreds of photos, and soon felt I understood the possibilities and how to attain them.

I finally bought Photoshop for my home computer and got to work. If I got stuck I'd go down to Digital Photo and ask the two employees, Johnathan and Melisa, for help.

One day, John, said, "You spend so much time here and DP is growing fast, I might as well hire you." I loved that job. I rarely got to work on the customers' projects, but I was the customer service guru – taking orders, opening the mail, watering the plants, etc..

John wanted a change. I helped him pack up the contents of DP and supervised the moving crew when we set up in the new location. About that time my John and I had decided to move back to Minnesota so my days at Digital Photo ended. They were good days but life goes on, We're pleased with our new adventure.

November 26, 2018

# ROBIN

I'm connecting with you from that place that my first human, James, told me about. He was right, it is a place in the sky that does have tuna fish bushes and catnip grass.

I lived for twenty good years. Twenty years of having a flair for individuality without (quite) becoming a feline diva.

One summer day I saw this scrawny boy walk into the Shelter. He was looking for a pet, and all the other cats put on their best shows of primping and flirting. I was little, and I knew I couldn't compete. When he finally noticed me in my little cage, I heard him say, "She's adorable but too small." That's when I reached a tiny paw out of the cage, touching his hand. I did it! I claimed my boy. Over the next two decades I realized I had also adopted James' entire family.

I loved my new home. I loved not needing a litter box. I was very discrete about my toilette.

I loved being able to explore the huge wetland behind the house. I could stalk my prey, reconnoiter, and investigate. But I did have to be careful of the fox family.

I loved escorting the whole family down the street to the Minneapolis Golf Club when they went for Sunday brunch. I'd be waiting for them under the bushes by the front door when they finally emerged again, and we'd all walk home.

When we went to Cotuit for the summer, I would walk to the beach with Mom and Dad. I'd duck behind shrubs when a car came by. If the beach was deserted, I'd sit on the seawall and watch my adults collect shells and polished rocks. It was a long walk home again, so I was really tired when we finally got back to the house—nap time!

I can nap anywhere … except in a car. When we moved to Florida or drove to Cotuit my vet would prescribe anxiety pills for the long car ride.

I could tell you more about my wonderful life, but now I think I'll take a nap.

January 28, 2019

# A IS FOR ADRIENNE, MY BEST FRIEND.

It has been a hectic, sad, happy, frustrating last month and a half.

I went out to MN for a week at Thanksgiving to see my good friend, Adrienne, who had been battling cancer for a year and a half (was given 6 months at the onset …). The day I arrived she had a seizure while at her boyfriend's granddaughter's Bat Mitzvah, and that really was the beginning of the end.

My being there was perfect timing because I have no life there beyond her and James, so I was able to be with her and even stay with her until we could get Hospice in place. She had planned on a big Thanksgiving feast with her extended family so I had ordered Thanksgiving dinner for two, for James and me, from Byerly's, the fancy grocery store in the area. It ended up that Adi was too weak to go out, so I upped the order to six. We had Thanksgiving dinner around her dining room table. Adi was able to join us.

John moved heaven and earth and flew up on

Thanksgiving day. Our six at the table were Adi, her son Chad, his girlfriend Cathy, John, James, and me. So very, very special!

Adi was at home the next week with round the clock care, was transferred to the Hospice house on Dec. 5th and died there with dignity and without pain on Sat. the 10th. We were in Minneapolis by Sunday afternoon. The funeral was Monday.

Adi had many close women friends. Her sons called us the Alpha Women. They asked us to be pallbearers because, "(I)t was the Alpha Woman who sustained her during her illness, it should be the Alpha Women who carry her out." A huge honor and one of the hardest things I've ever done.

John flew back after the funeral, I stayed there for the rest of the week. I spent a lot of time with Chad and Cathy and with Adi's younger son, Josh, who had come in from California. I saw each of the Alpha Women again at various times. We all really needed each other. Then back to Florida on Sunday the 18th. Into the museum for a day on Monday. And finally at home to get ready for the holidays. No time for a tree or decorations or cards (did get a wreath up outside), then off to LA on Thursday to be with Ed, Johanna, and baby Mary.

On Christmas day, we flew to Orlando to be with Geoff, Kellie, Jack and Katherine – and James, who'd flown down. We left LA at 8:30 am PST and got to

Orlando at 7:00pm EST (that three hour time change is a killer!) Stayed one night with them – did Christmas again, then drove to Gainesville. James was with us until Friday the 30th.

When I walked out the door to go to work on Monday morning (January 2, 2006). I thought, "Thank goodness, maybe we can get back to normal. It's time to re-enter the real world." Sadness still creeps in, but I'm ready to go forward. It's just a matter of how.

January 5, 2006

# VENICE IN THE MIST

The mist never lifted; it gave the city an ethereal light. Buildings seemed encased in glistening gray, bordering on white. It erased the centuries of grime; it hid the ravages of the elements, both human and natural. Seeing Venice for the very first time from the water through the mist was like seeing a place only dreamed of in fairy tales and romance intrigues. I fell in love instantly.

How often does one marvel at first impressions? They are powerful and they are lasting. Up close, Venice is like a lot of cities – a bit down at the heel, a bit worn out, old and pitted, graffiti laden, but I will always see it, in my minds eye, through that mist.

How can a city be built on an island not much (inches in some spots) above the sea? The water bus let us off near the square; the tide was lapping at our shoes as we hurried along the promenade. At high tide San Marco Square shimmers with water and reflects the buildings encasing it—a sight never anticipated.

# A Special Place

There's a very special place in my heart for my big brother. Rich is only four years older, but he has always been "bigger than life" to me. For many years he really *was* bigger, lots bigger. His size often intimidated me when we were little. Sometimes he would pin me down and tickle me. There were times he'd run after me on cold winter's days, scuffing his feet on the carpet, causing tremendous zaps when he finally caught up to me. Occasionally he'd just plain haul off and belt me. And I kept egging him on, coming back for more. I adored my big brother. And I detested him, too. Simultaneously!

Rich had some great friends on Glen Road—Jimmy Rich and Tommy Frost—and I adored them too. Rich and Tom came back from camp one summer with songs they taught their sisters, Nat and me. I remember the lyrics to this day, and if Rich had a better voice I'd ask him to sing along with me. I know better…

And speaking of singing, I always loved our trips to western Massachusetts to visit Rich at Mount Herman. (I'm not sure I ever forgave my parents for sending my big brother away, but that's another story…) Each year Mount Herman and their sister school, Northfield, would get together for a semi-religious concert. All students had to participate. When I finally found Rich in the sea of student faces I could see him joining with the others to make beautiful music. Later he told us he'd been asked to not sing but just to mouth the words.

I'm always so pleased when Rich remembers (it's probably Pam who does the remembering) my birthday and calls. But when he starts singing "Happy birthday to you…" I usually stop him. Being tone deaf when you love music must be painful!

Rich and I did have a love—hate relationship. As an adult I understand that that's normal and healthy. I will never forget that Saturday in the fall (sometime in the late fifties) when mom and dad got a phone call. All the officer would say was, "Your son was in a car accident and is at Newton Wellesley Hospital." Of course they asked, "Is he alright?" The reply was, "We can't tell you anything more right now."

As they sped off to the hospital they asked me to stay by the phone and take care of Bob if he got back from playing with his friend. I was all alone. I sat on my bed and worried—and cried—and worried. I couldn't stand the thought of my brother dead. I was shocked to think how I'd wished him dead on numerous occasions. I felt so guilty! I had the radio on and I really lost it when the song "I Never Felt More Like Singing the Blues" came on. "For I never thought that I'd ever lose..." To this day, if I hear that song, I remember vividly sitting on my bed and crying. I'm sure that was the day that I learn how closely aligned love and hate are.

Rich healed and life went on. I never felt like Rich really lived with us again when he left for Mt. Herman. He was home for the holidays and he'd be with us at the Cape all summer, but he lived out in the barn and other than mealtime I didn't see that much of him.

We did have a lot of good times though. I remember listening to Spike Jones with him. We'd get laughing so hard we could hardly hear the words. Then there was the time Mom and Dad bought him the Oscar Brandt record he'd asked for. They were horrified when they discovered that it was rather risqué (oh dear!) We liked the song, "Oh dear, what can the matter be? Seven old ladies locked in the lavat'ry. They were there from Sunday 'til Saturday. Nobody knew they were there..." Mom and Dad were soooooo disapproving!

Rich was amazing in my eyes. He was so accomplished. He wasn't just a scout; he was an Eagle Scout. He wasn't just a sailor; he was the commodore of the yacht club and came away from the Labor Day meeting each summer with armloads of silver. I always regretted not being a racer myself, not for the love of the sport but for the silver...

Rich was a marvelous gift giver. I must admit I was

really jealous when he'd find the perfect present for Mom and Dad. One year it was the cuckoo clock and for the 30 years that it hung on the wall, I was reminded each time it did it's thing, that it was the perfect gift and that my parents loved it above all others. It was Rich who gave me my first manicure set. (I'm sure he doesn't remember!) It was red lather and absolutely beautiful. I loved it.

I liked Rich's girlfriends. Having no sisters I glommed onto the older girls that visited. And then came Pam. She was pretty and feminine. She was sweet and kind to Rich's little sister. I adored her! She shared my room with me when she visited on the Cape, and I watched with wonder and awe as she'd prepare to meet the day. I loved her perfume and I saved and saved my meager allowance until I finally had enough to buy that same perfume. I didn't know about body chemistry then, and I was appalled to discover that that perfume just plain stank on me. Ah, life's lessons!

From the outset, there was no question in my mind that Pam was the right one! She and Rich seemed perfect together. So when they got married I was thrilled! (By this time I had a wicked crush on her brother, Bill, so the wedding was an agony and an ecstasy for me. Bill never did return my affection – in fact, though he took me to the Sadie Hawkins Dance [since I got up the nerve to ask him and he was polite enough not to say no], he spent the night dancing with his future steady girlfriend! But that's another story for some thing like "Life's most embarrassing moments."

I remember visiting Rich and Pam in Plymouth. John and I had been married for only a year or two. At one point during our visit we all went over to the park – Rich and Pam, the unbelievably adorable little girls, Nat and Holly, their huge, but sweet German shepherd, Schnapps and John and me. We flew kites and rolled in the grass and gave piggyback rides and frolicked in the autumn warmth. And I remember thinking, these are the best parents! My brother is a wonderful, loving father.

Life went on. We didn't see much of each other. Our visits stopped. We'd see each other occasionally when John and the boys and I visited mom and dad in Cotuit. But basically we drifted apart. I felt very left out of my brother's life. It hurt me to lose the closeness I thought we'd had – the sense of family, but I was never able to tell Rich how I felt.

And just when I thought Rich was pretty much out of my life, I went into the hospital with a blood clot. My dear, wonderful brother called me every single day! Every day!

And that's when things started to turn around. We became friends, not because we were brother and sister, but because we found we liked each other. I treasure that! It's tucked away with all the memories in that very special place in my heart.

Happy 60th Rich!

November 21, 2000

# PART THREE

# POEMS

# GRANDMOTHER

I sat at her feet

As she rocked in the chair

Brought back 'round the Horn.

Her gaze was distant

As she told of far off places

And of her grandfather's voyages

To capture the dwindling whales.

Places and stories she'd heard

At her grandmother's feet

So long ago.

"Saltwater runs in my veins,"

She told me.

"Never forget your past.

Treasure the lives that went before.

Listen well.

Learn.

Don't forget.

Saltwater runs in your veins, too."

September 2, 2000

# Breathe Little One

Breathe little one. Your journey is over, And I'm still
here.

I will feed you And care for you. I will protect you And
love you.

But I can no longer Breathe for you.

So, breathe little one. Breathe my son.

Breathe.

December 10, 2007

# Hearing My Just-Born

I remember hearing my just born son crying....

The nurse had wrapped him up tight and put him on my chest.

"Hush little one. I'm here with you."

"I will love and protect you."

"I will nourish you."

"I will introduce you to your family."

"I will guide you and teach you."

"I will treasure you always."

"Welcome to this great big, wonderful world."

August 30, 2022

# It Covers the Ground

It covers the ground like a loose fitting sweater And
    insulates all it surrounds.

    It is as soft as eider down.

And as white as salt-drenched sails on the horizon. It is
    as quiet as forever.

On a moonlit night it glistens—a million prisms
    catching the light. Each flake a piece of art unto
    itself.

Together they are a blanket of beauty. It does not last
    forever.

It disappears like sugar in your tea.

And you yearn for its soft, white, quiet beauty again,
    Next year.

January 11, 2023

# IF I RAN THE MUSEUM

If I ran the zoo
    Said young Gerald McGrew
I'd make a few changes,
    That's just what I'd do.

—Dr. Seuss

If I ran the museum
    Said old Beverly B.
I'd make several changes,
    And morale would be key.

I'd foster great teamwork
    And make everyone feel
That they and their feelings
    Were topmost and real.

August 8, 2006

# PART FOUR
# WRITING CRAFT

# WRITING GROUP

My writing group starts up again next Monday after a winter hiatus. I'm really looking forward to it. I've missed it and its writers.

Seven lovely ladies came to the first meeting over two years ago. "I can't write." "I'm not a writer." Each said, "But I'll try it." each decided. Only one didn't come back.

"Can you write?" I asked. "Pick up your pen or pencil and write something, anything." Of course, you can write! You learned in first grade, if not sooner. The pen/pencil and the alphabet are the mechanics of writing."

What have you written? Think about it. Grocery lists: Notes to self. Everyday type stuff. But more creative? Birthday wishes. Get Well cards. Notes to tuck in your kids' lunches, etc. Your messages are usually personal, well thought out and creative. Oops, there's that word, "Creative" Creative writing! Not so scary!

Lo and behold, all of them are writers—<u>creative writers.</u> We've been at it for a couple of years now.

We're happy and proud to be writers. It's hard work, but also great fun.

The best part is hearing what each of us has written from the assignment given the week before. They're not hard because there's no right way to do them. All I ask is that they write. At the beginning they were embarrassed to read their pieces aloud, but that's the beauty of the group. Each claims we all wrote on the same topic such as:

A quote; A bit of memoir; What does this picture say? What is your first memory?

The beauty is that each of us interprets the topic differently. And everyone does it <u>right!</u>

We're not writers? Oh, yes, we are!

March 19, 2019

# MY SEESAW

Since Jamaica and the writing course, I have been on a seesaw when it comes to my writing. Sometimes I've been UP and sometimes I've been DOWN. More down than up after the first couple of weeks back home. More up than down since I came to Cotuit and made a writer's pact with Pam to meet twice a week and produce whatever the assignment we'd concocted.

I loved that week in Jamaica. I loved the wonderful, supportive, interesting, interested, talented, perceptive, challenging, caring people I spent that week with. And I really loved realizing that I could, indeed, write. And write pretty well. I was really fired up.

On the trip home I was in a long line at the Atlanta airport. It was 11:00 p.m. and we were all trying to get to little, old Gainesville – not one of Delta's top priority airfields. I had plenty of time to strike up conversations with those around me in line. Everyone was grousing about his or her long day. All seemed to be playing one upmanship on how tired they were and how far they'd come and who was most tired, etc.

"So where'd you fly in from?" someone asked.

When I replied, "Jamaica" my line mates rolled their eyes and said sarcastically, "Oh that's too bad!" Not one to be dismissed, I said, "Oh, it was nice, but I was working, too." When asked what my line of work was I didn't flinch. I merely replied. "I'm a writer!" I was amazed at myself. They were very impressed. I was really UP.

Well, once back, I was a writer for the first two or three weeks. I wrote each morning for at least half an hour. I'd do a warm up exercise like Anne taught us. I'd journal a bit. I'd write opening sentences and so on, but I didn't write anything I really liked and I lost the little motivation I had. I missed the structure, the guidance and the wonderful feedback from my Jamaica trip friends. I decided I just couldn't do it alone. I was really DOWN.

I shelved the writing. I read books about writing and I kept a daily diary, but I didn't really write. Then I headed for Cotuit.

With fear and trepidation Pam and I decided to meet twice a week, every week. My seesaw was stuck in the middle. Could I write? Would I write?

The answer was yes. Yes, I could! Yes, I would! We took turns hosting our meetings. And we took turns coming up with assignments. One time we wrote a fairy tale. Another, a piece around the quote, "Nothing is accomplished without enthusiasm" (Ralph Waldo Emerson). Some pieces were lighthearted. Others were heavy. We tired writing in the 2nd person. We wrote a piece about someone or something special and from the piece tried to capture the essence in a poem. Miraculously, ideas for assignments kept popping up.

When we got together we'd read to each other. We were amazed at our abilities and our progress. Pam and I are very different writers. I could not write with her insights and flair for philosophizing in crisp, clear paragraphs. And she couldn't do my "the fewer words the better" style. We love and admire each other's writing and in the process celebrate our writer selves. Each time we meet we marvel at what we've done. I always leave our meetings with a smile on my face. Definitely my seesaw is UP.

But then the next meeting approaches and I haven't a clue how to tackle the assignment. I've thought about it over and over for the last several days, but I draw a blank. I go to bed thinking, well, it will come to me in the morning. Or, or I'll just have to tell Pam I couldn't do it. Then I'm DOWN.

But morning comes – pre dawn sometimes—and all those possibilities that have been zooming around my head the last few days seem to fall into place and I write happily, and seemingly, well. UP! UP! UP!

Occasionally I have read my work to John. He's very supportive and thinks I'm the next best writer after Shakespeare. But isn't it strange how sometimes our ears hear one thing and our hearts feel another. One of our assignments was to write a very descriptive piece. I wrote two-plus pages on Jingle Shells. I liked it a lot. So I read it to John. He listened intently and said, at the end. "That's fabulous, but you do know that thickness is not the same as density!" I was crushed. My heart forgot the "That's fabulous" part and only focused on the criticism. I was definitely DOWN, DOWN, DOWN. If my audience is to go beyond Pam, I'm really going to have to toughen up.

Now summer is over and fall schedules are upon us. Pam is back at school and will be Wonder Woman if she can tackle three courses and sustain this level of writing. I know that I still need the structure and camaraderie to accomplish anything. And I head back to Florida in a few weeks. I find the seesaw DOWN quite often these days.

We've vowed to keep at it over the winter. We'll continue with assignments – probably on a once a week schedule. And we'll work via phone. Long distance rates are pretty cheap if we dial before 8:00 a.m.

Seesaws are a lot of fun. Mine is basically UP.

September 6, 2000

# ON BEING CLEAR

Our language is a very tricky thing. May the reader, the writer, the speaker, the listener beware!

Earlier this summer I was enjoying a long phone conversation with a friend back in Minnesota. We'd been through all the kids and what they were up to. We'd talked about the past and about future plans to get together. Then she got onto the subject of her book club. She told me of how the couples had all met at a cabin up north for the weekend.

"It was so hot," she said. "We all jumped in the lake and Bob drowned." I was stunned that she reported this in such a lighthearted, off-hand way.

"That's terrible!" I stammered.

There was a long silence on the other end of the phone and finally she said, "Why? It really was hot!"

"But Bob drowned," I wailed.

She chuckled, "What I said was, 'we all jumped in the lake and bobbed around.'"

Horrifying for 30 seconds; funny in hindsight.

Years ago we were driving through an unfamiliar neighbor hood when we came upon a road sign – the usual yellow rectangle. It read:

## Deaf Child—Slow

My son looked over at me and said, "That's a mean sign, Mommy."

"Why do you say that?" I asked.

"Well, it's sad enough that the kid is deaf but why do they have to say he's slow too?" he replied indignantly.

That is what the sign said isn't it? Three little words. I had to explain to my son that the sign was there to warn us to slow down.

One of my favorite games as a child was "Coffeepot." I have no idea who named the game; it makes no sense. It could just as easily be called "Lawnmower" or "Nightingale." You'd take turns making up sentences using synonyms. Of course, at the time we'd never heard the word synonym. For example: "It was a 'coffeepot' day when we paid our 'coffeepot' to the bus driver to take us to the county 'Coffeepot.'"

What did "coffeepot" stand for? Fair, fare and Fair. Great fun to be the guesser. Great fun to be the maker—upper. Ah, childhood games!

It was Stendhal who said, "I see but one rule: to be clear." Our language is fun. It's complicated. It's ever-changing. And very often it is unclear. As speakers and listeners misunderstandings are bound to happen. Poor Bob! But for writers and readers there should be far fewer. What about a sentence like, "Live animals live in a zoo?" It takes a second to decide on "live" vs. "live." What about "I read the newspaper." Is that today? Or yesterday? Standing alone, you, the reader, have no idea!

Every now and then I have read something and ended by shaking my head and saying, "That was as clear as mud!" Directions translated to English from Japanese come to mind. Or newspaper columns that have obviously been clipped for space at the last minute and end up making no sense at all.

A writer needs to be careful. We need to know and understand the power of our language. And we need to know our audience. My description of the mudflats at low tide would be different depending on for whom I were writing. (Heaven forbid I end that sentence with a preposition "on who I'm writing for," hence the high—falutin "for whom I'm writing.") Consider writing about the mudflat for a scientist, a child, a mid—westerner, a Cape Codder. Hmmm.

The author must be clear not just about describing

things but also about describing feelings, thoughts, ideas, moods, and emotions. Writing is not an easy task. It takes precision, attention and care. Why write if your reader isn't absolutely clear about what you're trying to say? Be clear. Rise to the challenge. Write!

August 29, 2000

# THE SMELLS OF A CLAMBAKE

It's 7 AM. July. Onshore breeze is ruffling the bedroom curtains. The scrape of a shovel outside. Dad's digging a pit in the driveway. Cape Cod driveways are usually made of crushed shells, stones and anything lying around. So, it's not too hard to dig a round shallow pit about four feet wide. He'll line the pit with the large stones you picked up with your brothers along the beach. Dad told you to stay well above the waterline, so the rocks won't be soaked and explode when heated. He's going to lay a fire in the pit. He'll stack old cedar shingles and driftwood into a wooden tent. (He's a scoutmaster.) He'll light the fire at precisely eight o'clock. So, the first smell of the clambake is a wood fire.

Yesterday, we all went over to the head of the canal to collect seaweed, huge bags of it. The seaweed has a smell all its own. Definitely green, ocean flavored, and a bit of rot. Not so pleasant to most folks, but it's the second smell of a clambake.

By noon, the fire's heated the rocks. Meanwhile, you and your mom and brothers and neighbors have assembled the ingredients: Steamer clams, corn on the cob (which is soaked to ensure it cooks), and potatoes go into individual net bags. And of course, lobsters, which are naturally dark brown when they go in, but the familiar red when they come out.

Dad rakes the wood and charcoal away from the hot rocks, and the men throw the wet seaweed—bags and bags of it—to make a thick layer over the rocks. Then the lobsters and the bags go on the seaweed, and—quickly now—a big canvas tarp over the whole thing.

Then we wait.

Two hours later, maybe three, Family, friends and neighbors have assembled. One of the older gents pulls up a corner of the flap, inspects a bag, and nods. The men pull off the tarp and a huge cloud of steam escapes. It carries a distinct perfume. Stink, to be honest. But a beautiful thing. That's the third smell of a clambake.

It's time to eat. You take a paper plate and stand in line. There will be a lobster, steamed clams giving off an almost-sweet hint of the sea, corn, and potatoes. Butter in a cup. That delicious, melted butter is the fourth smell of a clambake.

There will be tables and chairs for the older folks. The rest of us hunker down on the grass and consume the feast. When we're finished, stuffed to the gills, my grandmother would say, the paper plates, lobster and clam shells, corn cobs and lots of greasy napkins go into barrels. Next day, someone takes the whole mess to the dump. That's the last smell of the clambake, one which we don't dwell on.

July 2023

# JINGLE—JUST SO

You may not know this, since you're only human, but Jingle shells are very athletic. We can run and jump and do somersaults and backbends and handstands. We're really quite amazing. Maybe you'll be lucky enough to see for yourself some day, but probably not, unless you're a very small child.

We haven't always been called Jingle shells, you know. Why, there was a time when we were called Toenails. Now really, who wants to be called a Toenail? We're very glad we were renamed. Want to know the story?

It happened not so long ago, not so far from here. We lived on an island, a little slip of an island. It was very close to the mainland. In fact, it was so close that at low tide it wasn't an island at all. It was a peninsula. It connected to the mainland at one end. Pretty neat, don't you think? An island that becomes a peninsula for a few minutes, twice a day.

Our island was deserted (and we liked it that way) but we enjoyed watching people at the beach across the way. Everyone loves the beach. Especially the children.

Their gaiety and zest remind us of ourselves. They, too, run and jump and turn cartwheels.

But on with our story. One day, while most of us were lazily lying in the sun, we noticed a family across on the beach. We're always quiet when there are people around, but sometimes our little ones get antsy. At any rate, the little girl must have spied the occasional backflip or somersault. She just wasn't sure what she'd seen. She wandered off for a closer look, and because it was low tide, she came onto our island.

We stayed very still as she approached. She lay down to get a closer look at us. She took such delight in our colors, shapes and sizes that our wee ones soon began to show off for their visitor. They jumped and flipped and carried on. The girl loved the show and giggled. Soon the little ones, both shells and child, fell asleep.

But heavens! The girl's family was frantic. They discovered the little one was missing and were running and calling to her up and down the beach. How could we help them we wondered. "Simple," I said. "We'll call them!" And I laid out my plan.

Soon we were all doing our very best gymnastics. All at once. We brushed against one another as we cartwheeled, "Jingle." We met in mid air as we did handsprings, "Jingle, jingle." We pushed off of one another as we flipped about, "Jingle, jingle, jingle." Our chorus sang out, "JINGLE! JINGLE!"

It was the boy who heard us. He waded across to the island and found his sister. He gently woke her and called to his family. Everyone wanted to know what had led him to the island. "I followed the sound," he said, "the jingles." Of course the adults didn't hear a thing, but the boy and his sister smiled as they looked down on us. "These are Jingle shells!" they said as they pointed to the quiet mound of shells at their feet.

August 9, 2000

# The Blueberry Muffins

Ralph Waldo Emerson once said, "Nothing is accomplished without enthusiasm." He should taste my blueberry muffins.

It was a glorious summer morning. Blue, blue sky. Crisp and dry. The kind of day you dream about during the sluggish winter days. Josie and Pete were up already despite their late evening and they were arguing about who had blown the best bubble even though they knew they were not supposed to chew bubble gum before breakfast.

"Come on kids," I said, "We're going to make blueberry muffins."

They came running, bright with anticipation until I added, "Get on your shoes. We have to go pick the blueberries." I wonder if Mr. Emerson heard their moans and groans. He'd definitely turn over!

At least the dog was happy! She bounded along in front of us, pleased with her freedom. The kids (and I, I must admit) nearly jumped out of our skins Gertie flushed a pair of quail. Their swooshing wing beats startled us, to say the least.

Pickings were slim. It would seem that the birds had tackled the bushes, enthusiastically, before we arrived. But there were enough for muffins. After all we only needed one measly cup. So we set to picking. I realized too late that I shouldn't have brought the kids out without something to hold them over. Every blueberry Josie or Pete found its way into a mouth. I could see I was on my own. One cup turns out to be a heck of a lot of blueberries.

The trip back down the path was serene until Gertie, off in the woods, started barking. Pete went to investigate before I could stop him. "Gertie's found a box turtle," he called back. "Can we keep it?"

"No, it would miss it's mother," I replied. Turtles miss their mothers, I thought. Now that's lame! It was then that I realized that Pete was knee deep in poison ivy. "Get back on the trail, Pete," I hollered. You and Gertie will need a bath as soon as we get home."

What would we do without the outdoor shower I wondered as I scrubbed my son's legs and corralled the dog long enough to wash her down too. Of course I ended up wet enough to have justified putting on my bathing suit for this ordeal. But no. I would have to drip dry.

"Okay kids! Let's make muffins!" I enthused.

"Can't we just watch Nickelodeon while you do it?" Josie asked.

"No way, missy," I answered, trying hard, very

hard, not to sound annoyed. "Wash your hands. I've got a job for you." And I set her to sifting the two cups for flour. I won't bother to describe the mess. Suffice it to say we had flour everywhere!

Meanwhile I had Pete working to break one large egg into the bowl. Simple? Not so apparently. Several pieces of egg shell found their way into the bowl, and as I pulled them out I tried to remember the horror stories Id' read about egg shells in some women's magazine, some months ago… Next I set Pete to measuring a half—teaspoon of vanilla.

"This smells so good," Pete said just before I saw him upend the bottle and take a swig. "Blah!" he yelled as he spit the foul tasting liquid onto the counter top. "That's why we add sugar to recipes that call for vanilla," I instructed. But I think it fell on deaf ears.

There were no more mishaps before all the ingredients were safely in the bowl. Josie was able to line the muffin cups with paper baking cups and Pete was able to do the mixing. Thank goodness the batter is supposed to be lumpy.

I did let the kids watch Nickelodeon while the oven did its thing. I needed a few minutes with the paper and a cup of coffee. Those 20 minutes were the fastest of the morning I realized as the buzzer sounded. Were the muffins golden brown? You bet.

The kids came running at the sound of the buzzer. It was hard to convince them that they really had to wait a few minutes to let their muffins cool. I told them that the blueberry juice was still boiling. Did I lie?

Finally I gave the kids the high sign and we settled down to a wonderful breakfast. For the first time all morning they were very enthusiastic!

"Want a blueberry muffin, Ralph?"

August 21, 2000

# What Am I Doing?

What am I doing? What have I done?

As she rushed to the gate she wondered if this trip was a good idea. Am I nuts? Curious? Hopeful? Insane? After all she hadn't seen Hank in thirty-plus years. They'd been high school sweethearts. Destined to marry and live happily ever after.

Well, that didn't happen! He left her for a cute cheerleader in the class below ours. I countermanded by hitching up with an idolized football jock in the class above us. He was handsome, but dumb as a rock. I was so glad when he graduated and went off to Podunk U on a football scholarship. Oops, careful what you wish for… I found myself alone in my senior year. None of the guys in my class were interested in me. We were finally the upperclassmen.

Upperclasswomen were now "used goods."

So now I'm off to reconnect with Dustin. I knew his wonderful wife had died a few years ago. Our class is good at keeping track of us. When he called the other night, he said he'd learned from a classmate of my David's passing last spring and he wanted to reach out to me. We kept in touch for this last year. In one call he suggested we get together. He lives near our hometown and the idea of going home yanked at my heart strings. So, we made plans. And here I am at the gate…

Yes, this was a good idea! A very good idea indeed! We had a lovely weekend. We've had many more since. After a year we got tired of travelling back and forth so we've rented a house down the street from our old high school (which is now the towns senior center). And Yes! This is our happily ever after!

October 28, 2019

# SHE STEPS OUT

She steps out into the silky, starlit night but feels only terror. It is balmy, but she shivers and pulls her arms about her. "Where is he?" she asks herself again and again. "Where is he?"

He'd said he was going to study with a friend – that he'd be back by 10:00. At 11:00 she'd called the friend's house. No, he'd let awhile ago.

How many scenarios could she conjure she wondered. Was he drunk or stoned or both? Was he frolicking under the covers with his latest? Was he joyriding through the countryside? Was he on his way to the police station in the back of a cruiser? Was he in an ambulance on his way to the hospital? Was he being transported to the morgue?

How many emotions could she run through? Fear escalating to terror! Disgust building to anger! Love bordering on hate! Hate rebounding to love!

Headlights! He pulls into the driveway too fast. The brakes squeal. Her handsome young son smiles as he casually makes his way toward her. She strains to hear if he slurs his words as he says, "Sorry I'm late. I stopped to help an old man fix his flat tire." He winks as he brushes a kiss on her cheek. She smells Bianca.

How many questions could she ask?

How many lies would she get in return?

"Get to bed, we'll talk in the morning," she says.

She's too uptight, too jittery to go to bed. She picks up her favorite pen, smooths out a sheet of paper and begins to write. She remembers having read, "we do not write in order to be understood, we write in order to understand." (C. Day Lewis)

July 2000

# THE PHONE CALL

"Hello, Betty! Finally!"

"Oh, hi Shelly. I haven't heard from you in ages." (Damn. Why did I answer the phone?)

"Well, I've called a few times." (And I know you have caller ID!) "How are you, Betty?"

"I'm fine. And you?"

"Oh, fine. Keeping myself busy!"

"Really? Whatcha been up to?"

"Well, ever since the break—up I've been making myself get out and do things. It's been awful."

"Yeah. The split must've been hard. Sorry I haven't been much help to you in that department. I've been really busy myself." (If you only knew.)

"Which reminds me, I hear you've been seeing Paul." (You bitch!)

"Really! Well, I have seen him around town a few times. Ran into him just the other day at the grocery store." (Not to mention in the movie theater and the bowling alley and most recently, his bedroom!)

"Susie made it sound like you were dating or something."

"Really?" (Wait 'til I get my hands on Susie.)

"Well, are you?"

"I wouldn't really call it dating," (It's way beyond that!) "but as I said I have run into him a few times."

"That sure makes me feel better. I didn't think my best friend would shag my boyfriend without at least talking about it. Thanks for reassuring me."

"No problem, Shelly. I gotta run, I'm expecting company any minute. Let's talk again soon."

In the background, Shelly hears a familiar voice call out. "Hiyah, baby! How's my girl?"

"Shhhhh!"

"Oh my god!"

CLICK!

CLICK!

September 12, 2000

# THE BOOK WAS ALL THE RAGE

The book was all the rage that summer. Everyone was reading Anne Morrow Lindbergh's *A Gift from the Sea*.

She realized now that she'd read it too young. She'd thought she was a grown up—a woman—after all, she'd been pushing twenty. And this was definitely a woman's book, she realized when she reread it twenty plus years later.

During that first read she'd found it boring. She'd thought from the title that there would be more about the sea, the beach, marine life, but no. There were a few shells mentioned in passing but few of those were found on her local beach. Then Lindbergh would get off the subject of shells and into descriptions of her husband, her home, her children, the changing times. It really had been a dull read, although she'd never said that out loud. After all, the book was that talk of the town and Anne Morrow Lindbergh was practically sainted.

She'd picked the book up again last summer and, if she hadn't known better, she would swear that it had been rewritten. It was beautiful, poignant and so wonderfully true. It flowed, and soothed and made her sigh – ah, yes.

The book hadn't been re-written; her life had been written. That first time she'd read it she was only near the end of chapter one. Many chapters had been added, the ones about marriage, financial restraint, career 1, career 2, child 1, child 2, move 1, move 2, move 3, empty nest, financial freedom, and so on. There were chapters yet to be written but the ones completed had been well lived, she mused.

*A Gift from the Sea* should be read and reread and read again. She now sees it as a treasure – a treasure she'll hold off sharing with her daughter for a few years yet. It all comes down to something Anne Morrow Lindbergh penned so long ago – "Woman must come of age by herself." Yes! Many times – in many ways.

August 15, 2000

# INQUIRY BOX INTRODUCTION

*(Bev wrote this piece to introduce the program she led at the Florida Museum of Natural History in Gaines-ville. Teachers in elementary and middle school could request the program. Bev usually took the rolling suitcases that contained the program to the schools and other venues and often presented them herself.)*

Have you ever held a one to three thousand—year—old tool in your hand? Have you ever learned how snakes rub their heads on something rough to start the shedding process, and then picked up a snake shed and examined it from head to tail, seeing its various kinds of scales and even the spaces that were around its eyes? Have you ever "seen" the difference between warm blooded and cold blooded animals by using a strip thermometer?

Well, you have if you're lucky enough to be a school child (or a person of any age visiting a community center or library) in Florida. Opportunities for hands—on learning and fun abound with the Florida Museum of Natural History's "Inquiry Box—Museum on the Move" program. The Inquiry Box (IB) program takes the educational power of the Museum—its collections and research findings—into the classrooms and other centers of the surrounding communities. In so doing, it reaches students and others who may be unable to make the trip to the Museum.

The Inquiry Box (IB) program was developed in the late 1990s. The Education Staff at the Museum saw the need to create object—rich educational lending materials on a variety of topics that could be used by teachers in their classrooms. They intended the IBs to be presented by well trained docents who know the material well and enjoy being out in the field. Many ex—teachers find this a perfect way to take the skills they learned in the classroom and their love of the Museum beyond the exhibit halls.

Each of the seven Inquiry Box subjects was developed for specific grade levels. All of the IBs used the Florida Sunshine State Standards when assembling the materials, and all were designed to enhance preparation for the FCAT, the state's testing program.

For Kindergarten through 3rd grade, there are the "Florida's Reptiles and Amphibians" and the "Florida's Butterflies and Moths" Inquiry Boxes. Third, 4th and 5th graders have three IBs designed for their studies: "Northern Florida's Early Native People," "Southern Florida's Early Native People," and the "Seminoles of Florida." For 5th through 8th grades the IBs are: "Florida's Fossils" and (still being developed) "Florida's Geology."

The staff and docents have found that the topics are broad enough and the hands—on material is interesting enough that all of these Inquiry Boxes can be presented anywhere to any age person—Head Start to nursing homes and all in between. In this respect, the IBs are a lot like the Museum itself.

So, what is inside the Inquiry Boxes? Each box occupies two suitcases or a duffle, and each has a Museum-developed Teacher's Manual (which will soon be posted on the Museum's website). There is a selection of age appropriate books, as well as reference books that help the teachers and the learners. There are laminated word cards that help with concepts and new words for each topic. For example, in the Native Peoples IBs, there are cards for "paleoindians," "archeology," "midden," and several other important words. There are games, laminated maps, pictures, and large artifacts and replicas. All of the replicas are made by the behind-the-scenes scientists at the Museum.

Finally, there are the pouches (14 in each IB, which can serve as many as 28 students) filled with artifacts, replicas and activities. Each pouch in Native People, for instance, has one celt, the everyday tool used by the early people here in Florida. Each of the celts is the real thing! People love that they can feel and hold this stone artifact; they can't help but compare their celt with their neighbors' celts since each is one of a kind. There is a life size replica of the catlike figure that was found on Marco Island during an archeological dig in the 1800s. There are two or three points in each shared box. Kids (and adults) always want to call them "arrowheads," but they learn that there were many different uses for points and again, they love to compare theirs with their peers. These points, too, are artifacts—"the real thing," kids like to say. There is an activity in each box to show how the native people made cord, rope, etc. The students (and adults, as well) love the challenge that the strands of fibers present, and many do devise ways to make a strong cord that doesn't break or unravel.

The presenters usually don't have enough time to cover everything in the Inquiry Box, but that's not a problem because the teachers can keep the IBs for up to two weeks as long as they are willing to return them to the Museum. Oftentimes, the teachers have never been to the Museum, and they are glad for the opportunity.

The Inquiry Boxes are wonderful because of the really exciting materials the Museum can provide. Equally important are the docents who make the presentations. They bring skills, knowledge and commitment to the IB experience. The combination is an outstanding program that greatly enriches our communities.

# WRITING RULE # 9

When I first started following Julia Cameron's dictate in *The Artist's Way* to write three pages each and every day, I became a dedicated writer. I read all the things various writers recommended to their readers: we would-be writers. Most of the things I read are shortened and listed on the "The only 12 ½ rules you'll ever need" handout.

I did read all the rules writers are supposed to follow, but they started to be redundant, therefore boring, and finally easily forgotten. I guess I wasn't a true believer yet.

My very beautiful, leather Coach pocketbook was really heavy on my shoulder before I put anything in it. I then added my wallet, a checkbook, a change purse, credit cards, a lipstick (or three or four), a hairbrush, a ring of keys and various treasures the boys asked me to take care of while they ran onto the Little League field, and on and on. Soon my shoulder was screaming at me. Needless to say, adding a notebook to this collection was not on the top of my list! I did have a pen down in the depths of the bag.

One day I was riding the bus from Boston to the Cape. All of us Cape Codders much preferred the bus to driving ourselves. Battling Boston drivers is a pure nightmare, and nowhere is the traffic more horrific!

I do love the ride. The bus is sleek and comfortable and best of all most of the bus divers will tell you that you may not talk on your phone except to call your pick up person after we've crossed the Cape Cod Canal. So civilized!

It's great to be sitting above all the cars. There's so much to see on the two-hour (with stops) trip. First the city, then the suburbs and finally the countryside. I always found a window seat on the right side so I could lean my head against the window and take in everything along the way. I would daydream about who might have lived in that old house or if anyone had ever recently walked through the dense forests we rode past. How did they dig the wonderful Cape Cod Canal back in the '30s? Who designed and built the two majestic bridges that connected the land. I remember what fun it as to see the railroad bridge drop down so the trains from Boston, New York and Providence could get to the Cape. Once train had passed over, the bridge would go back up so the ships could pass through. The canal passage meant that ships didn't need to battle the Atlantic and go far east in order to head southwest to head down the coast. There had been many shipwrecks in those treacherous waters before the canal was built.

I thought of when I was a child and there had been a devastating fires burning on the mainland north of the canal. The forecast was for heavy winds and the dire prediction that the fire might jump the canal. The Cape was a tinderbox. As a six-year-old, I was terrified.

As we neared the canal, I realized, I had so many things I could write about. Yikes! I needed to write down all these ideas (even that word reminded me of a story!) I knew I had a pen, but paper? No! I quickly pulled out my checkbook and wrote down all my many musing on deposits slips. Now, I always carry a notebook of some sort now and I've given up my lovely patinated Coach bag for a practical, lightweight Bagallini.

February 11, 2018

# ONCE UPON A TIME

Once upon a time in the far off kingdom of Cumberland, there lived a beautiful princess. One day her father said to her, "Dear, sweet, Anna, it is time for you to marry. We must find you a husband worthy of being king."

"Yes, your majesty," replied Anna to her father. But what she was thinking was "I must find a husband worthy of my love."

Word went out through all the lands that the princess was to be wed. Men appeared from all corners of the world hoping to win the hand of the king's beautiful daughter.

Anna was unimpressed as she met with the various suitors. After each long day of being presented with various prospects, Anna would head to the stables to escape the court. She would ride like the wind through the woods, up the hills and around the valleys with her dear friend, Jack. She'd known Jack since they were children. He was the stable boy then. Now he was the stable master, a job he'd earned through hard work, great care and sincere love of his work.

When Anna complained to him about her suitors, Jack would question her. "What about Charles XXIV?"

"Too silly!" Anna replied.

"Well, how about Lucius?" asked Jack.

"Too pompous!" said Anna.

"There's Dirkweed?"

"Too boring!"

"Henri Claudius?"

"Too sad."

And so it went. None of the young men, so far, suited Anna. There seemed to be no one, but her father was determined. Soon he chose Marcus the Seventeenth to be his daughter's mate.

"Marcus the Seventeenth?" wailed Anna. "I cannot marry Marcus the Seventeenth! He hardly knows I exist. He spends all his time with you. He laughs too hard at your jokes. He's always by your side, but behind your back I see him sneer. He doesn't care a wit about me, father. He pays me no mind."

"Hush, my daughter. Marcus the Seventeenth is a good and honorable man and you shall be wed. I'll hear no more of your childish blabbering." And word went out throughout the land.

Anna spent more and more time at the stables telling Jack of her woes. He tried to assure her that love could grow, that the world would be bright, that her life would be happy. But finally he decided he must try to help the beautiful Anna and he went to the king.

"Ah, Jack, my boy, what a fine young man you have become. I value your service to my court and you enduring friendship with my daughter. How may I help you?" asked the king,

"Your majesty," Jack began. "I have come to ask you to reconsider your choice of husband for Anna. Marcus the Seventeenth is not worthy. He is a toad in a long line of toads."

"How dare you!" bellowed the king. "Off with you. I will not have such disrespect in my kingdom! Be gone!"

Sadly, Jack did as he was bade. But before he set out he found Anna and said to her, "You will wed Marcus the Seventeenth. Be as loving as you can be, and if that fails you, pretend that you are with me. I love you, Anna. I always have and I always will."

The wedding took place six months later. There was much fanfare and great celebration. Jack arrived at court disguised as a handsome young prince from a far off land. He was given a front row seat. He watched lovingly as Anna, looking tired and alone, walked down the aisle with her father. Waiting at the altar, Marcus the Seventeenth sneered,

The ceremony droned on and on and Anna's eyes and mind wandered. Soon she's caught the eye of a dashing young man in the front row. She smiled. As the ceremony was ending, Marcus the Seventeenth whispered in her ear, "Do not kiss me, dear wife." But as the archbishop said, "You may kiss the bride," and Marcus the Seventeenth bent forward to brush her cheek, Anna thought of Jack and kissed him full on the mouth.

POOF! Much to the astonishment of all in the great hall, Anna stood alone. And there at her feet was an ugly, warty toad.

"Jack was right!" bellowed the king. "Find Jack!" he commanded.

"At your service, sire," said the young man in the front row as he moved to stand beside Anna. "In my banishment I established a new realm which my people and I have named New Cumberland in honor of you, your majesty."

"You are a man worthy of being king," proclaimed the king.

"And you are a man worthy of my love," said Anna, taking Jack's hand.

The ceremony began again. And this time when the archbishop said, "You may kiss the bride." the couple embraced and kissed a sweet, dear kiss. With that the archbishop said. "I now pronounce you husband and wife."

No one noticed the ugly, warty toad hop off into the garden. And everyone lived happily ever after.

July 2000

# The Power of the Pen

She remembered sitting on the back stoop with her father. She asked, "What are you doing Daddy?"

"I'm writing out an assignment for my students at the College."

"What's an assignment?" she asked.

"An assignment is what I ask my students to do before our class meets again the next time."

She could see he was making very pretty letters. Prettier than usual. They must be very important, she thought. She had learned the ABC song when she was very young but she couldn't read yet.

Her father was using a shiny blue pen. *A* different pen than she was used to seeing.

She recognized most of the letters when she saw them and asked, "Daddy, what does that say?"

"That, my sweetheart, says something very big even though it takes very few letters to say it. It says,

***'The Pen is the Tongue of the Mind.'* "**

"What does that mean?" she asked.

"We'll save that for another day, dear one, but now I must finish my work and you must go help your mama set the table. Off you go."

When she started school, it didn't take her long to learn to read. She loved being able to read books by herself, but she loved still more snuggling with a parent while being read to. Reading felt good, but being read to felt even better. In first grade every kid had a desk with a round hole in the upper right corner.

She wondered about that until one day Mrs. Devereaux brought out little jars she'd filled with paste (the kind of paste half her schoolmates thought was delicious. Blaaaa!) They fit in the holes just right!

She learned to write in first grade, too. She had to use a fat pencil and fat crayons, but no pens. No pens?

It wasn't until fifth grade that she could use a real pen at school. Yay! And that's when she finally learned what those holes in the desk were for. They were inkwells! Those same paste jars were filled with ink. *They had a cap.*

She would write and write until her pen ran out of ink. She loved to fill it. The pen had a little lever on the side that pushed down on a little sack inside the pen. When the lever was up she'd put her pen, pointy end in the inkwell, then slowly turn down the lever. The pen would fill with ink and she'd write again. Her <u>father</u> gave her first pen when she was in third grade. She'd learned all about pens and ink from him. By sixth grade she had several pens. She carefully filled each with a different color ink.

She finished school, went to college and tackled adult life.

She was never without a pen. She kept a journal. She carried a little notebook everywhere she went. She didn't want to miss anything. Her children, grandchildren and someday—great grandchildren would learn about the past from this woman of the future.

She wrote and wrote and wrote. She loved the feel of a pen and the magic that flowed from it. It felt like all she had to do was think and the words would appear.

"Yes," she thought, that's what Horace meant when he said *The Pen is the Tongue of the Mind.*

# My Shore Bird

She flitted down the beach lightheartedly. How fast those little feet could carry her. She played with the waves. She would follow the water as it receded then skitter back up trying to beat that next one. She'd lower her head daring the waves to catch her. Every now and then she'd poke into the wet sand. What treasures did she find?

Life seemed good as she continued down the beach pausing occasionally to look back to see where she'd been, how far she'd come. Then she'd turn back, repeating her game.

I sat quietly watching, transfixed by her spirit and whimsy. There were others like her, but I took great joy in singling her out. She seemed so special, so unique. I loved the freedom, the poise, the sport, the boundless energy. I marveled at her – such beauty in Nature.

I continued watching. Now and then I was afraid she'd get too far down the beach, but to my delight she'd turn back toward me and continue her pattern. A part of me wanted to join her, but I knew my presence would end her dance along the waves. I didn't want that. I watched, impressed by her small, well-preened body. I was struck by her single-mindedness. I marveled at those tiny feet – so fast, so capable, often barely touching the ground. I had to smile.

But I was gently jostled from my reverie when she called, "Mommy, mommy, may I go in swimming now?"

"Ah, yes," I mused, "My daughter is also a fish!" And I happily got up to join her at the water's edge.

August 18, 2000

# EYES AND EARS

They have been apart for far too long. They will not be allowed to be together for long. They must make the most of this time. Could they be suspended in it? They will try. Their embrace is happy and sad at the same time. They want to feast their eyes on one another, but the embrace is too powerful, too hard to break. They stand there, wrapped in one another's arms. Her face tells of her joy and her sorrow. His face, bent into the nape of her neck, can only be imagined. They are surrounded by riches, wrapped in a golden robe, amid golden swirls. Like the gold, their love is precious; like the swirls, it is full of energy. At this moment they are at peace.

Can you see this couple I've been writing of? Can you imagine the space they occupy? Can you visualize their love? I hope you see, for I count myself a good writer.

What I have been describing is a painting by Gustav Klimt (1862—1918). I treasure this painting. It speaks to me. I have no doubt that Klimt, who died several generations before I was born, wanted me to hear its

tale. This wonderful painting hangs in my bedroom –
the only *right* room in the house for it, I think. The
painting says to me, this is the place of love, of joy, of
warmth, of sexuality and sensuality. If I could be
suspended in time, this is the place I would choose.

Gertrude Stein once said, "A writer should write
with his eyes and a painter should paint with his ears."
How true. Usually we think just the opposite; a writer
writes to be heard and a painter paints to be seen. And
certainly that *is* true, but a good writer thinks in terms
of what a reader sees as well as hears. A good painter
thinks in terms of what a viewer hears as well as sees.

I have done little research on Klimt's work. I have
no idea what he really had in mind when he created *my*
painting. I don't think that matters. It tells me a story. I
*see* it and *hear* it as I have described above. Each
viewer may look at it and see and hear a slightly
different story. That's okay. In fact, that's the way it
should be.

I want my readers to hear what I write, but I also
want them to see what I'm writing of. If I write, "there
was a green tree" readers can conjure up all sorts of
green trees, but if I write, "the tall, snow—dappled pine
stood out against the steely blue sky" the reader has to
narrow his or her vision. There is always some room for
interpretation. Isn't that why most people, if they have
read a book, prefer it to the movie version most of the
time. Why, isn't it true, that even in nature, you can

stand side by side with someone and still see the scene both of you is staring at a little differently. Thank heavens for individuality.

I would modify Stein's suggestion just slightly: writers should write with their eyes and artists should create with their ears. And I would add: readers and viewers should use their eyes and ears to make the most of what they hear and see.

October 3, 2000

# Never Underestimate

Never underestimate the power of a smile! Webster's defines "smile" as a "noun: a grin; a facial expression in which the corners of the mouth turn upward, usually indicating pleasure." The dictionary points out that "smile" is also a verb and that this English word comes from the Middle English (1250—1300) *smyllen*. But the good book does not speak to the power of the word.

Stop reading. Close your eyes and picture some of the precious smiles you have seen over the years. Chances are you are smiling at your recollections.

I see the smile of satisfaction on my son's face when he finally hit the baseball.

I see the smile of gratitude and relief on a student's face when I gave her a chance to write her own paper rather than handing in her brother's work.

I see the smile of encouragement from my father as I tried repeatedly to learn to whistle.

I see the smile of my friend across the room when our shared secret gives silent understanding.

I see the smile of victory on the Olympian's tear streaked face as she listens to her national anthem.

We think of smiles as showing joy and happiness, but there are smiles that hurt. I see the smirk of the class bully as he heads toward me in the empty hallway.

I see the smile pasted on of my friend's face. She's petrified to stand in front of the city council and give her impassioned speech. Speaking of petrified, I remember seeing a complete stranger suddenly smile as I walked into the office of my new job that first day. What an ice-breaker. Smiles can be wonderful tension erasers.

What about those "most embarrassing moments?". Usually there is someone sensitive and caring nearby who flashes you a smile and eases the mortification. And the others, smiling, laughing at you are usually doing so just because they're so glad they didn't do what you just did.

Then there are your own smiles. Remember! There's the smile of self satisfaction. The smile of self approval. The smile that says, "I can buck myself up!" There are your own smiles of acceptance, of gratitude, of gratification.

Do you know what the longest word in the English language is? It's "smiles" because the is a mile between the two esses. Do you know the song, "Let a Smile Be Your Umbrella?" Are you getting a little tired of the round, yellow Smiley Faces®? What about, "Say cheese?" Now, that causes a *really* unnatural smile!

So, there is power in smiles. We feel their power

each and every day in many ways. It seems that smiles beget smiles. Offer a stranger who sneezes on the sidewalk a "God bless you!" and you're bound to get a smile in return. Powerful!

But I've saved the best for last. It's the power of the smile of love. Look into the eyes of your lover and spouse, your children and their children. The smile that is generated comes from deep within. It is sweet and warm and wonderful. It says, simply, but with electric power, "I love you."

Smile.

September 21, 2000

# KEVIN

Kevin had the feeling that this wasn't going to be just another ordinary day. After all, it was his birthday. He had been waiting and waiting for this day. He wanted to be grown up. He liked the double digits!

But something was different. When he looked in the mirror he realized he would have to shave! To shave? And look how big I am, he thought. I really am a man. Wow! Zowie! What a birthday!

Kevin found a razor in the medicine chest and proceeded to shave with ease. When did I learn to do that, he wondered. When he in his closet he realized that all the clothes there were big! "Killer sport shirt! You really have great taste, Kevin!" he said as he slipped his hairy arm into a sleeve. He headed downstairs.

"Happy birthday, dear," his mother said as he walked into the kitchen. "I know it's your birthday, Kevin but why are you dressed so casually? Aren't you going to work at the bank today?" she asked.

"Oops!" Kevin replied. "I guess I got carried away. It's not casual Friday, is it!" And off he went, back upstairs to change into one of his several boring, three piece suits."

Driving the car was a snap. Kevin was amazed at his driving skills, and luckily this spiffy Mustang seemed to know the way to the bank. Kevin found his desk and began tackling the tasks at hand. The work wasn't hard and his abilities were exemplary, but Kevin had a hard time focusing as he stared outside at the cloudless blue sky. He couldn't help but think of riding his bike to the park for a pick—up game of baseball.

The phone jarred his thoughts and he picked it up. It was his mother asking if he'd please stop at the grocery store on the way home to get a few things. It seemed strange to Kevin that he even had to buy his own birthday candles. That's not how it's supposed to be!

The grocery store was crowded with the after work crowd trying to get dinner organized. Several women had unhappy, tired children in tow. They'd obviously just been picked up from daycare and wanted to get home. Kevin filled his shopping basket with his mother's requests and waited in the long line at the "10 items or less" counter.

When he pulled into his driveway he noticed a car parked in front of his house. He walked in to find Diana talking with his mother. He'd known Diana since grade school. He'd had a crush on her in fourth grade.

"Hello, darling!" she said in a raspy, very feminine voice. "How's my birthday boy? Wasn't it nice of your parents to invite me for dinner. I just love celebrations!

How about a birthday kiss!" is said throwing her arms around him.

Yikes! This was too much! He thought. What now?

"Kevin! Kevin!" He heard his mother's voice. "Time to wake up, sleepy head! I thought for sure you'd be up by now considering what day it is!"

"Wwhaaaat? Oh! Thanks for waking me, Mom. I was having such a horrible nightmare!" Kevin said as he bounded out of bed.

He had the feeling that this wasn't going to be just another ordinary day. After all, it was his birthday. He was ten!

October 12, 2000

# FRIENDS

They were inseparable. They met when they were four and a half years old and they really connected. Her name was Sara; his was Will. Sometimes they played at her house, sometimes at his. Sometimes they'd play outside and their mothers would sit nearby, keeping an eye out and gabbing. They became good friends too.

Will and Sara were never at a loss for something to do. They built "houses" using leaves for the walls and room dividers. They were very upset if someone entered their house other than by the door. Sara had lots of dolls and Will had many stuffed animals. Their family was big and very well cared for.

Now and then Will would come home a bit down. "Did you have a good time at Sara's today?" his mother asked.

"Oh, it was okay." He said dejectedly, "Sara wanted to play house and she was going to be the Mommy and I was going to be the Daddy."

"Well, that sounds like fun," said his mother.

"Well, it was boring. Sara got to do all the fun stuff and she made me sit on the couch pretend to drink beer.

She said that's what her dad does. Boring!"

Will wanted only two things for Christmas that year – a three piece suit like his own dad's and a Barbie doll. He got both and used each lovingly and well.

Will loved to wear that suit, and wear it he did. Luckily it could go in the washer and dyer. And he and Sara spent hours with their Barbie dolls. They'd dress them for all sorts of occasions and both mothers pitched in my sewing and knitting clothes for the various Barbies.

When it was time to go to kindergarten, Sara and Will were pleased to be in the same class. They'd head for the bus arm in arm and return at noon happy and looking forward to an afternoon of fun. Often one or the other mother would feed the two of them and they'd continue their fun non-stop. Every now and then on weekends they'd even have a sleepover.

In first grade they still played quite often. In second grade they got together now and then. Still the best of friends but now their circle of friends expanded and started to exclude the opposite sexes. Will and Sara were still friends but they tried not to let the rest of the kids know it. By junior high they really avoided one another. Sara would walk home from the bus with the girls. Will and the boys would walk home on the other side of the street.

In high school Sara became a cheerleader and a member of the popular girls club. Will was a good student and a good athlete. He was liked and respected but he didn't run with the "in" crowd.

One day it got back to him that Sara was spreading the word that Will used to play with dolls. Will took Sara aside and asked her to cool it. She laughed in his face. He was sad and mad. Sad to lose his old friend and mad to find this new, mean spirited person.

One night, soon after that, they were at the same party. As Will walked by a group that included Sara someone tittered. "I hear you really dig Barbies, Will."

"Yeah, I did." he answered and started to move on.

"Sara says you really got into dressing and undressing those dolls," another piped in.

"Hey, cool it you guys. So what if I played with dolls when I was a kid." he replied. He was starting to get really annoyed.

"Sara says you really liked those big titties."

Will looked over at Sara. She was grinning at him with a "gotcha now" grin. He had had enough.

"Did she also tell you that we've slept together?" he asked. "Many times." he added as he walked away to the sound of stunned silence.

January 15, 2001

# MY BIG SISTER

My big sister is everything to me. She's my guide, my confidant, my teacher, my inspiration and my friend-my best friend.

My sister seems to know everything. Everything about me for sure. She knows when I'm up and when I'm down. I can ask her anything and she will have the answer. I can tell her anything without having any repercussions.

She's a wonderful listener. She lets me rant, she lets me cry. When I am angry she seems to know it even before I understand why. When I'm hurt she comforts me. When my feelings are hurt she does the same.

When I'm happy my big sister smiles with me. If I am sad she cries with me.

When I'm on top of the world she shares the spot with me.

And when I'm down in the dumps, she's there beside me bucking me up.

If I do anything that is nasty or hurtful, or self-serving or mean she guides me through to better thoughts and prompts me to make amends to anyone I've hurt.

She has made me into person I want to be-caring, loving, helpful, kind. She holds my hand and guides me on my way.

# BIG GAME

"Hey, Billy, that was a really exciting game." "How can you say that Mom? We lost!

"Yes, I'm sorry, but it was a well-played exciting game on both sides. I hope you had fun playing.

"How can I have fun when we lost?

"You know, Billy. In all team sports there's always a winner and a loser.

"So how can it be fun when you lose? I hate soccer. I never want to play again!"

"Sweet Billy. You know what your Dad would say if he were here. 'Stop your blubbering. You're a big boy now.' I agree with Dad, don't you?" (Be a big boy now, but I also think it's okay to cry from disappointment. After all you are only 6. The *way* You play is more important than winning. I also know that you did your very best. Don't beat yourself up, Billy."

"But Mom! My very best wasn't good enough. The field was slippery from all the rain."

"It was just as slippery for the other team." "But losing still hurts!"

"Yes! But as Dad would say, "Shake it off."

"Billy, let it go! Let's have a snack. And don't forget what Annie knew: The sun'll come out tomorrow!"

# THE SHOULDS IN LIFE

One day I heard my neighbor say, "I have decided that I am not going to should on my head anymore." I was about to chuckle—I could have sworn she'd said, "shit on my head." I stifled my laugh, however, knowing I could not have heard that. Mrs. Bigelow never used four letter words; I doubt she ever used "damn or "shoot." So I said, "Pardon me?" And she repeated, "I have decided that I am not going to *should* on my head anymore."

I have never forgotten her declaration. I thought of it often as I raced around as the mother of three, teaching full time and working on my Masters degree, trying desperately to get the *shoulds* of my life taken care of. I should do laundry, today. I should spend some time with my mother-in-law. I should send out Christmas cards *before* Christmas. I should spend more alone time with my husband. I should! I should! I should!

Each year, as I grow older and approach the age Mrs. B. was when she made her declaration to me years ago, I try harder and harder to take her decision as my own. She was right. She was so right. There are just too many *shoulds* in life.

I've come to see that there are degrees of *should.* For instance, there are the *shoulds* of necessity that are usually *musts.* I should shovel the driveway. (Yes, it must get done if we're to get anywhere today, but what I *could* have done was gotten the boys to shovel the driveway!) I should get home and get dinner started. (Yes, my family must have three square meals a day, but I *could* have spread this burden: "You cook tonight." or "Please, pick up take-out on your way home."

There are the *shoulds* of obligation. I should stop and vote on my way to the dentist. I should send a sympathy card to my colleague. I should be sure my kids understand the value of money.

And there are the *shoulds* that are really *wants.* I should walk through the Nature Center. I should take a long, relaxing, hot bath. I should read Jane Austin again. Those are the *shoulds* that often aren't acted upon because of time constraints or other *shoulds* of necessity and obligation.

To be fair, a lot of *shoulds,* are *wants* even if they are also necessities and obligations. Sometimes I did love bundling up and enjoying the peace and quiet of shoveling the soft, beautiful snow. And certainly I wanted to feed and care for my family. I did want to vote. Of course I wanted to teach our sons the importance of values. As a teacher, I wanted nothing less than that my students love learning.

And I did want to be with my husband away from the hustle and bustle of life.

I went through many years of my life trying to be superwoman – super-wife, super-mom, super-daughter, and super-teacher. And when I fell short I was super guilt-ridden. The problem, I see now, is that there wasn't and still isn't enough time for all the *shoulds, musts* and *wants* in life. You must be selective.

I'm so glad Mrs. Bigelow said to me, "I have decided that I am not going to should on my head anymore." I know now that she meant that you have to give yourself permission to give up the *shoulds* that aren't wants and not feel guilty about it. I can give up the should of baking, the should of reading X because Y liked it, the should of saying yes to this request or a committee. I can simplify my life. Enjoy life. Mrs. B. was a wise woman, and I'm getting there. With more practice I *should* make it!

January 14, 2017

# How to Attract a Girl

*A seventeen-year-old girl advising her fifteen-year-old brother in the art of attracting a girlfriend.*

Joey, c'mere. Sit. I'm gonna tell you in very short words so you can understand how to ask April out. I know she turned you down for the sock hop, but you gotta understand, that wasn't a refusal.

Uhh … yes, I know she said no, but it wasn't, like, a real no. It was the beginning of a negotiation.

No, it's not the United Nations or anything. But I am, after all, more experienced than you. Two years older, and everybody knows girls are smarter about this stuff than boys. So, she's in your math class, right? Is she smart or dumb?

Okay, since she's smart, you just happen to walk out of class beside her and ask about something in math class. Don't play dumb, just a comment, like "that last problem was tricky" or something. That'll appeal to her.

She's a cheerleader, isn't she? She'll know you're a basketball jock, but you can remind her. "Looking forward to the Edina game?" Just make it indirect.

Then, once you're talking, ask her to get a soda or something. Not a direct ask, just a suggestion. You will need to read the situation. If she says, "I'd like that," and smiles, then you can make a date. If she says, "Sure," and kind of blows you off, well at least you've put down a marker. This is a long-term project, y'know.

Hey, Joey. Hear you're going out with April tonight. Good for you. You can thank me profusely every day for the next week. A cash treat wouldn't be out of the question.

Of course. Glad to advise.

Most important thing on the date … Ask questions, show interest in her. Like, how's that adorable little brother? Something to get her talking about herself. It's okay to show her pictures on your phone, but otherwise, keep it in your pocket. If she stops talking, or you can't think of anything to say, you're going to want to grab the phone. That'll make her grab her phone, and you might as well flush the date.

What are you going to wear? Really? No, you can't go as you are.

First off, take a shower, but none of that smelly body wash you guys seem to like. And lose that holey sweatshirt. I know you love it, but she won't. You need to be just dressy enough to show you thought about clothing at all, which is a compliment to her, but not over-the-top pressure to impress. Shorts are okay. How about that polo shirt Aunt Bee gave you for your birthday?

Comb your hair.

And while you're making faces in the mirror, make sure there's no spinach on your teeth.

# YOU HAVE NO IDEA

Julie Burroughs pushed through the revolving door of the bank, fingering the stack of bills in her pocketbook. After the shock of Uncle Bill's death and the bigger shock of inheriting fourteen million dollars, she had been pondering what to do. For some reason, before the bigger issues overwhelmed her, she wanted a stack of cash. She never carried much, always using her credit card, but it wasn't much of a kick that the same old blue and white Visa could probably buy a small airplane. Not that she wanted one. So, on her lunch break, she went to her bank—not the ATM, inside—and drew $1,000 in fifties and twenties.

The feeling of elation lasted through giving a twenty to a homeless woman on the Mall and until, lunch break over, she returned to the IDS and her cubicle. Then the weight of her situation reappeared as a band of tension running across her upper back.

She had never really thought about what it would be like to suddenly have more money than she could imagine. She remembered reading somewhere that people who won the lottery often didn't change their life much. Was it that they couldn't imagine anything different or was it that they were happy and didn't want to change? Not that it had mattered to her. She never bought a ticket. Now she understood. They were no longer invisible.

She guessed she was lucky that way at least. She was still invisible to the rest of the world when she wanted to be. No reporters were going to track her down. The news of the bequest was private. Only the lawyers involved and she knew the details, and the lawyers were in California. But speculation saturated the funeral, and news finally leaked. Bill had been the family black sheep, disowned by his father after they came to blows over his future. He was exiled to California in the early days of the technology boom. He'd made a fortune in venture capital. Julie had always adored Bill and refused to cut ties with him when the rest of the family did. No doubt Bill thought he was doing right by the only one who had loved him unconditionally, maybe relishing the irony just a bit. But it divided the family into the unhappy wing and the jealous wing, with Julie at the intersection.

Charlie Rollins leaned over her partition. "I got a meeting upstairs at 3:00. Drink after work?"

"Sure." She felt a little flustered, like she always did around Charlie. Flustered in a good way.

And he was gone, striding down the corridor toward the elevator, whistling out of tune, broadcasting positive energy and friendliness. Julie thought again that she might just love him. Of course, her father would never approve of her marrying a black man, and that would add another dimension to the tension in the family. And why was she suddenly thinking marriage?

She forced herself to go back to work, but then was grateful to have the simple, reassuring logic of a ten-page spreadsheet to keep her anxiety at bay. She had almost relaxed when the others on the floor began drifting toward the elevator. Charlie must be finished with that meeting.

The Local was full of the usual youngish crowd when Julie walked in. She spotted Charlie talking with a colleague, walked to him and gave him a kiss on the cheek, but more than just friendly. He looked a little surprised and gave her a radiant grin.

The bartender slid drinks for Charlie and his friend and took her order for a Remy Martin, water on the side. She slid the Visa card across the dark wood. Charlie gave her that little half smile that forced a shiver down her spine and said, "Big spender, huh?"

She said, "You have no idea."

Not that she thought of herself as invisible. She wanted to be visible in good ways, honorable ways. But most of the When she was young, she had become fascinated with the stories of J.R.R. Tolkien and his life as a scholar of languages at Oxford. She remembered how quaint, but somehow charming that in later life, when the *Lord of the Rings* became popular, the poor-as-a-church mouse Oxford don was delighted to purchase a new vest but otherwise led a life largely unchanged.

Like her mom's friend Lucille, who had confided that her husband Harold seemed to have lost interest in her. Lucille became more and more unhappy and finally, over breakfast, blurted out, "Harold, you never tell me you love me anymore," and broke into tears. Harold snapped down the top fold of the Star Trib and peered at her, shock on his face. "I said I love you when we got married, Luce. Nothing's changed." She wondered what Harold would do with fourteen million dollars.

October 2022

# THREE GIGANTIC WORDS

Her two grandchildren, Ben(6) and Susie(4+) were happily playing with Legos on the floor. *Yes,* she thought, *I can finally get lost in my book again. Ahhh!*

It wasn't long before Susie started wailing and throwing Legos at her brother.

"I can't do this! Ben can, but I can't," Susie said between sobs.

*So much for getting lost in this book,* she thought.

"Patience, little one," she said. "Patience means being able to accept or tolerate delay, or trouble, without getting angry or upset. Ben, would you please show Susie that she really can do this."

"She's such a baby," he said.

"Ben, you couldn't do this at her age either," she said. "Have you ever heard the word *compassion*, Ben? It's another big grown-up word. Compassion means being concerned for the sufferings or misfortunes of others. Your sister is suffering right now. She feels helpless. Show her that you understand how frustrated she is. Show her your compassion. Please help her."

Grandma continued, "Here's another big word for

you: *Simplicity.*

It means easy to understand or do. You two get back to your Legos, I'm going in to rustle up an afternoon snack. Good luck, Ben! Good luck, Susie."

"Grammie, I did it. Ben showed me."

" 'We knewed you could did it.' That's what your daddy said to me many years ago when I got a knot out of his shoelace. Now go wash up, I've got cookies and ice-cream for you. Your mom will be here in a few minutes. And remember those words you learned today. They are very special. You will teach them to your own grandchildren someday.

**Simplicity, patience, compassion.**

These three words are your greatest treasure.

April 7, 2019

# AUTHOR BIOGRAPHY

Beverly Anne Boden was born in Weston, Massachusetts in 1945. Weston was then a countrified town next to Newton and Wellesley. Her father's family had lived on Cape Cod, in or around the town of Barnstable, village of Cotuit, since the 1600's.

Bev's bio is woven into her writing, so it seems appropriate to integrate that writing into her biography. Read the stories in "Growing Up" to learn about her early years. She graduated from Weston High School, where she was editor of both the newspaper and the yearbook. She should write the rest her bio, part of which she did for her fiftieth Weston High reunion in 2013, for which she developed the class website. Here are her answers to the questionnaire she designed:

*What did you do in the first 10 years after graduation?*

I spent four years in Boston at Wheelock College with many weekends in New Hampshire or NYC. Graduated and got married a week later. We to a four-week honeymoon camping across the country—a great way to really get to know the person you've decided to spend your life with. It'll be 46 years in June.

I have come to really appreciate the unconventional way

Wheelock trains teachers. Few methods courses, but lots and lots of time in the classroom. Wheelock's reputation has served me well.

*And then what?*

We settled in Oak Park, Illinois, the first suburb west of Chicago. We were there for the 1969 convention. We watched parts of the city burn when Martin Luther King was assassinated. I taught for two years in Oak Park and was asked by the principal to welcome the first African American student to my class. The kids and I really liked this addition to our classroom. The faculty was not pleased. Our neighbor put a For Sale sign up on his front yard after the word got out. I'm happy to report that Oak Park has since become a model city for integrating without a fuss.

When I became pregnant with our first child, I had to resign from teaching. You couldn't even look pregnant in those days. Geoffrey was born in 1969.

Edward came along in 1972. When he was just twelve days old, we packed up and moved to the Cape to start a boatyard with my brother. Eight months later we returned to Illinois, and John resumed working for Belden Corp. While we were away, the company's headquarters had moved west of the city to Geneva, today considered a suburb, albeit a long way from downtown. We felt isolated because public transportation didn't come out as far as Geneva and the gas crisis made driving anywhere a luxury. After nine years in Illinois, we decided to move back east. John's job search of east coast companies found him the perfect job. One tiny hitch … it was in Minneapolis. We packed up again and moved northwest.

The day after we arrived in St. Louis Park, Minnesota, Geoff went into first grade. All the neighborhood kids were so welcoming and helpful. We have never regretted that move.

Minneapolis is a wonderful city. The chain of lakes within the were preserved by a forward thinking man, Theodore Wirth. So although there are mansions across the streets from the lakes, there are foot paths and bike lanes that connect them, beaches and sailing in the summers. Ice fishing, skating and cross country skiing on the lakes in the winter. Hard to describe, come visit.

James came along in 1978, so I managed as best I could with three males and a spayed cat. I couldn't stay away from the classroom and soon became the volunteer who never learned to say no. Even was nominated for Minnesota Volunteer of the Year.

When James went into 3rd grade I was hired to teach 2nd grade in his school. At first he thought it was cool that his mom was nearby, but soon he ignored me. The next year he went to our "paired" school, 4th, 5th and 6th. I taught 2nd grade for four years, then I too went to the higher grades. Taught 4th grade for two years. In the process I learned a great deal about computers—Minnesota was way ahead when it came to technology. So when our school librarian left I was hired as the Media Technology Specialist. That summer a new space was created at our building. It housed all the books but also had a computer lab of 30 Macs. Each classroom had at least one computer and we had a cart of "portables" that could be rolled from room to room. This was 1989!

Classes came to the lab once a week. I taught these kids how to make a data base, a spreadsheet, and to draw and paint. I had a much harder time with the teachers. They were "too old" to learn this new-fangled stuff. I finally told them I would not longer send out paper memos; if they wanted to know what was happening, they had to look at their email. Got to spend lots of money on books each years. Had two assistants who could fix any computer problem. I loved my job! But in 1997 we moved to Gainesville, Florida—center of the state, University of Florida, *Go Gators!*

John ran a couple of start-ups with university scienty scientists who had a product but no business skills. I got a job at the Florida Museum of Natural History in the Education department. Ended up being in charge of the outreach program, writing curriculum and amassing artifacts, touchables, models, bones, etc. that I could wheel out to a classrooms in a giant suitcase. Another job I loved.

*How have you changed since 1963? How are you the same?*
In the end, it was the kids I taught and their love of learning that stays with me. The best honor I've had—beyond awards and special recognition—was to come back to visit in friends in Minneapolis several years ago and have six former second graders take me to coffee—and to find that five of them have become teachers. The other is working on her masters in Elementary Administration.

Winters in Florida were wonderful, but summers… luckily

we could spend them on the Cape. But we missed snow! And winter! Geoff and Ed are on opposite coasts, James is here in Minneapolis, so when we were finished with the businesses we moved back to the Twin Cities. Condo living agrees with us. Don't even have to shovel! We call our top floor home our aerie. We're in the trees with the birds and flying squirrels. They visit our windowsill each evening. They seem to be as entertained by us as we are by them.

Bev's bio would not be complete without discussion of her family's history on Cape Cod. Her grandmother, Clara, wrote a novel, The Cut of Her Jib, based on her whaling captain grandfather's logbook, which she found in the attic of the family home. Cape Cod Life magazine did a long article on the book in 2012, when Bev republished the 1953 Putnam's edition. The article was based on an interview which is presented here slightly edited for clarity and length.

## The Cut of Her Jib Interview Questions

*Please state your name (as you would like it to appear in the story), your place of residence, your occupation, and your relationship to the woman who wrote the diary and to her husband.*

Beverly Boden Rogers. Summer: Cotuit, Mass.; winter: Minneapolis, MN; occupation: retired school teacher and media specialist. I am the great-great granddaughter of the diary's author and her husband. (Granddaughter of Clara Nickerson Boden).

*Why did your family decide to republish the book?*

We had several requests for the formerly out-of-print book. Not only is it a good read, but also a book of valuable history. The book was first published in a limited edition of 350 copies by the Cotuit Library Association with the support of Sidney and Mary Kirkman, who hired Gordon Grant and Walker Cain to do the illustrations. The commercial edition of 1953 was published by Coward-McCain, Inc.

*What kind of interest has the new edition drawn?*

There has been considerable regional interest in the book. We expect to travel north from Florida to the Cape starting May 8th, stopping at nautical museums along the way to introduce the book. We expect to be in Cotuit to introduce the book to bookstores, regional museums and some gift stores on or about May 15th.

*How would you describe your (grandmother), Clara Boden? Did she ever talk to you about writing the book or about her grandparents and if so, what did she say about it/them?*

I think she was a woman before her time. She was college-educated and quite independent. She gave me my first copy of Cut of the Jib on my 10th birthday. She was proud of the book and said she was very close to and proud of her grandparents, Faith and Seth. ('Faith' and 'Seth,' the names Clara gave her grandparents in the book, are used throughout this discussion. Faith was Clarissa in life, and Seth was Horace. – ed.) She spoke of sitting at their feet, spell-bound by the stories they told. When my parents went away she would stay with us. She didn't like to cook (after he retired, Clarence did the cooking) so every night we would have hamburgers. The first night it was a treat, but after a few nights it became boring….

*Does the house in Cotuit still exist? Where, exactly, is/was it? Did you ever visit it? Were you brought up on the Cape?*

It exists, so added-to and modified as to be unrecognizable. It is the big, boxy, white house on Ocean View Avenue in Cotuit. It overlooks the Sound, just before Ocean View drops down to the public Loop beach. Much as I've wanted to all these years, I have never been inside. (Note: Bev and John were invited to visit in 2018.)

The year I was born (1945), my parents bought an old Cap'n's house on the corner of Main and Sea Streets in Cotuit. I have spent every summer of my life but one in Cotuit. We were brought up outside of Boston, so were able to spend time with my grandparents and great grandmother in Cotuit on week-ends off and on throughout the year. My grandfather, Clara's husband, Clarence, died when I was six. Both of my brothers, Richard and Robert, live in Cotuit. John and I bought a summer home there in 1998.

*Where is the diary now? How long is it? Do you have any excerpts/transcripts from it?*

We have the original, which is quite fragile and faded. In the late 1940's, my grandmother undertook the task of transcribing the diary to typed text. It was a labor of love. The old spidery handwriting is difficult to read. Her intent was to publish the transcription. She once told me that transcribing the diary brought back many memories of those conversations with her grandparents. Her mother, Ina (the daughter-in-law of Faith and Seth), was still living then and confirmed many of Clara's recollections. In the early '60's, when copying was difficult, Clara's son, Marston (my father) was able to get the original diary copied, at fairly great expense. We may be able to lend a copy of that to you, but the transcript is far easier to read. We are trying to locate the transcript, which we hope to scan. One way or another, we think we can get you a copy.

*What were Faith and Seth Bassett's real names, and is the photo of them genuine? Was your great-great grandmother really born in Mashpee, to then become a teacher in Cotuit?*

Faith was Clarissa Bassett, and Seth was Horace Nickerson. The photo is genuine, and we have the original. Clarissa was born in Marshpee (now Mashpee, thanks to the New England accent) and became the first female teacher in the Cotuit school.

*Is there anything further you would like to add?*

With the proceeds from the sale of her book, Clara boarded a tramp steamer in New York City in December 1955 and traveled to Lahaina, Hawaii, the port of call for whalers in the 19th Century. She had always wanted to visit the whalers' community since hearing of it from her grandparents. All of us went to New York to see her off. She returned in March 1956. Grandmother took some Cotuit Atlantic water to Hawaii where she dumped it in the Pacific.

She told us she had thought of her grandfather as her ship made its way through the Panama Canal.

And finally, a part of Bev's biography straight from her great-great-grandmother's recipe book, passed through from her mother, the *real* clam chowdah:

# Quahog Chowder

1 Small piece salt pork cubed

12 large quahogs

Juice from clams

2 medium onions sliced diagonally

3 large potatoes cut into small chunks

Salt and pepper to taste

Large can evaporated milk

Quart milk

Butter (about ½ a stick)

Bottled clam juice if needed

Large bay leaf – optional

Cook salt pork until brown. Remove crispy pork bits but leave the fat. Add the onions – cook until clear, do not brown them. Add potatoes and juice – if more liquid is needed add bottled clam juice and/or water. Cook until potatoes are soft. Chop clams and add. Boil for 5 minutes. Never boil again – it will curdle. Add evaporated milk. Let cool. Add about a quart of milk after base is cool (1 to 2 hours). To serve, add butter and warm, being careful to not allow the chowder to boil. Serve with pork bits and oyster crackers.

Optional: Put 1 tbsp. fresh lemon juice into each bowl before filling with chowder.